"Puppies. You gav

Ah, so *that's* who this was. It was hard to recognize at first because Cay Emerson was one of the sweetest, kindest women Meg knew. The man in front of her had Cay's charcoal-colored eyes and dark brown hair, but she certainly couldn't tell if he possessed Cay's warm smile.

"Good morning to you, too, Grant."

His only reply was to deepen his frown.

Meg pulled in a breath. "I did not give your mother the puppies. She was there when we found them."

"But you talked her into taking them home." It was more accusation than statement.

"Oh, no," Meg refuted. "Taking them home was all your mother's idea."

He crossed his arms over his broad chest. Even out of uniform, the man radiated law enforcement. Cay hadn't mentioned he was coming or why, but Meg got the sense Grant Emerson never did anything without a very good reason.

Allie Pleiter, an award-winning author and RITA® Award finalist, writes both fiction and nonfiction. Her passion for knitting shows up in many of her books and all over her life. Entirely too fond of French macarons and lemon meringue pie, Allie spends her days writing books and avoiding housework. Allie grew up in Connecticut, holds a BS in speech from Northwestern University and lives near Chicago, Illinois.

Visit the Author Profile page at LoveInspired.com for more titles.

RESCUE ON THE FARM

ALLIE PLEITER

LOVE INSPIRED

INSPIRATIONAL ROMANCE

LOVE INSPIRED®
INSPIRATIONAL ROMANCE

Recycling programs
for this product may
not exist in your area.

ISBN-13: 978-1-335-93177-1

Rescue on the Farm

Copyright © 2025 by Alyse Stanko Pleiter

Love Inspired
22 Adelaide St. West, 41st Floor
Toronto, Ontario M5H 4E3, Canada
www.LoveInspired.com

Printed in Lithuania

MIX
Paper | Supporting
responsible forestry
FSC® C021394
www.fsc.org

He that dwelleth in the secret place of the most
High shall abide under the shadow of the Almighty.
I will say of the Lord, He is my refuge
and my fortress: my God; in him will I trust.
—*Psalm* 91:1–2

For CJ and Emily

As they start their life together

Chapter One

Meg Kittering watched the enormous dark-eyed man yank open her diner door and then practically fill the doorway. He scanned the Sundial Diner until he found her. Glaring in a way that somehow made his eyes even darker, he walked straight to her.

"Puppies." He muttered it in the same tone Mike the cook used when he burned the bacon. "You gave Mom puppies."

Ah, so *that's* who this was. Now she saw the resemblance clearly. It was hard to recognize at first because Cay Emerson was one of the sweetest, kindest women Meg knew. You couldn't get a more different personality on a similar set of features than the man in front of her. Grant Emerson had Cay's charcoal-colored eyes and dark brown hair, but she certainly couldn't tell if he possessed Cay's warm smile.

"Good morning to you, too, Grant." She pushed cheer into her voice that wasn't exactly genuine. This morning had been a battle to get her five-

and six-year-old daughters to before-school care. The refrigerator was starting to make alarming noises, and there wasn't money to fix it. There was barely money for anything, for that matter. If she missed another mortgage payment, things were going to get dicey. She'd need a quart more coffee before doing battle with the likes of Grant Emerson.

His only reply was to deepen his frown.

Meg pulled in a breath. "I did not *give* Cay the puppies. She was here when we found them."

"But you talked her into taking them home." It was more accusation than statement.

Meg doubted anyone ever talked Catherine "Cay" Emerson into anything. Cay was also the sunny brand of stubborn Meg's late husband often attributed to Meg. Cay's faith and generosity made her a fixture in the small, tight-knit Montana community. Meg admired her and was pleased to call the woman both a customer and a friend.

"Oh, no," Meg refuted. "Taking them home was all your mother's idea. Nearly instantly, I might add."

He crossed his arms over his broad chest. Even out of uniform, the man radiated law enforcement. He was probably an excellent police officer down in Billings. There surely couldn't be enough crime and mischief in tiny High Mountain to keep him occupied here. Cay hadn't mentioned he was coming or why, but Meg got the sense Grant Emerson never did anything without a very good reason.

"I don't have time for this. I'm only here for a quick weekend visit, and now she wants me to help." He seemed irritated that no one had consulted him on the matter.

Meg reached for the coffeepot and one of the extra-large mugs she kept under the counter. She drew on the last of her usually vast stores of good nature. Why was helping his mother such an issue? "They were all so adorable. Except the littlest one didn't walk so well, bless him. She probably only needs your help to take them to your cousin Vicky's veterinarian office."

He nearly flinched at the word adorable, but Meg filled the mug and slid it toward him with a smile anyway. It wasn't a hard guess that the man took his coffee black.

"This won't be just a quick trip to the vet," he groused. "We both know what these puppies have started. I need to get back to Billings soon, and now that's going to be harder than ever."

She did know what the puppies had started. Meg just couldn't see why Grant was thinking of it as such an obstacle. "Why are you suddenly against your mother and her sisters starting Three Sisters Rescue Farm?" she asked in the face of his dark look. She couldn't afford to be irritating customers at the moment, but he really did strike her as someone who needed a serious attitude adjustment. "Your mom's been talking about this for ages, and now she's finally doing it. I love the idea."

"I just came up to check in on her. This isn't… I don't have the time to help her with this right now. I can't be up here all the time with this rescue-farm business. I've got…things in Billings that need my attention."

"Did she ask you to come up and check on her?" Meg countered, thinking a son should want to come visit his mother, especially if that mother was a woman as delightful as Cay Emerson. "I'm sure she welcomes your help, but I think Cay and her sisters can pull it off. Beautifully."

Grant huffed. Then he seemed to realize what his comments sounded like, pushed out a breath and sat down on a counter stool. "Look, I *do* care. I worry about her there all alone." He ran one hand down his face, and for a moment Meg saw a storm of conflict in his eyes. "I actually came up to try—again—to talk her into selling the farm. And now this whole puppy thing. She's…thinking with her heart, if she's thinking at all."

Selling? Cay selling the farm? She can't. Meg

had never told Cay that she cherished the idea of buying the farm when the woman was ready to retire. She lived right next door, and every day she saw the sun come up over that farm, she dreamed of moving herself and her girls onto it one day. Setting up a home in the white house with the big porch and spending hours in the red barn. Taking over the rescue farm from Cay someday made the dream even more wonderful.

Grant couldn't talk her into selling now. Not when Meg had no hope of being able to buy it yet. Right then she made a commitment to help Cay fend off Grant's "sell now" campaign, which had the happy benefit of endorsing the puppy adoption. If Meg could handle two feisty young daughters alone, she could surely stand up against the gruff giant currently drinking her coffee. "I think it's great—brave, even—to keep the farm," she declared. "I get that it will be a challenge."

"Challenge?" He bristled at that word. "Come on. It's unrealistic. Unreasonable."

"You don't believe God can call us to do such things?"

"No, I don't."

"Well, your mother does. In fact, she used the word 'ordained' when she saw the puppies."

He grunted. "Abandoned puppies are not a sign from God."

Spoken like a man who'd either lost his faith or never had any.

Which was he?

This trip had been a tough mission from the get-go, and seemed like it was only going to get worse.

Grant had come to town hoping to finally convince Mom the farm was too much for her. When Sergeant Atkins all but commanded him to take two weeks of vacation, coming up to High Mountain was the best option. But no way was he staying here two whole weeks. A long weekend at best; then he'd go back to Billings. Show back up at the police department despite orders and clean up the mess that had gotten him sent on this ridiculous mandatory vacation in the first place.

And now there were puppies. Adorable, needy pups that would guarantee Mom would refuse to sell the farm. The dogs were just the start. Soon there'd be other animals, and all kinds of maintenance, and expenses for the rescue farm.

The woman in front of him got a spunky, defiant look on her face. Under any other circumstances, he might find it amusing. Charming, even. But at the moment, it was simply exasperating.

"Honestly," she declared with one hand planted

on her hip, "I don't know why you're so worried. Seems to me, the woman who raised you can handle anything."

Grant didn't know what to say to that. No one gave him back talk like that at the department. People were slightly afraid of him, and that was how he liked it. His six-foot-five size and gruff demeanor kept people at a useful distance. They rarely argued with him. Certainly none of them ever looked at him as if he were a giant, wild mustang someone needed to tame for his own good.

"If you're looking for someone to help you talk her out of it," she went on, "you won't find it here."

Grant thought back to the skills he'd been forced to learn in his last conflict-resolution class. The class he'd had to take when he'd let his temper get the best of him. He'd said things no one should say to their commanding officer, even if said officer was flat-out wrong and refusing to do something about the corruption no one admitted was everywhere. *Engage*, he remembered. *Get on their level*. He forced the usual command out of his voice and tried to sound agreeable. "Okay then, how about some breakfast?"

Her face warmed with a great big smile. "Well, you should have led with that, sunshine."

He hadn't remembered Meg Kittering looking so pretty in high school. Of course, she was married—widowed, Mom had said—with two girls now. Did he look as different as she did? He surprised himself by hoping Meg didn't remember the grumpy, gangly teenager he'd been back then.

"Haven't had enough coffee yet," he offered in apology. It usually took more than a bit of coffee to get Grant anything close to cheerful. Sarge had referred to the enormous thermal cup Grant brought to roll call meetings as his "human juice." He wasn't that far off.

He had stormed into the diner in full confrontation mode, hadn't he? When did that ever solve anything? His tendency toward confrontation was what had landed him temporarily exiled from the department in the first place. Still, his brain kept shouting, *I don't have time for this. I have to get back and get someone to believe the crimes I've seen.*

She kept up the smile he didn't deserve as she refilled the large mug. Grant had to admit, it was really good coffee. "Another cup might be a good place to start. I tend to find folks more cheerful after a cup of coffee. And breakfast. You haven't ordered yet."

"Three eggs—fried, not runny—toast, and hash browns if you've got 'em."

"Of course we've got 'em," she replied. "It's one of Mike's specialties."

"Okay then, hash browns." He was actually pretty hungry. And under-caffeinated. Bad combination.

She wrote down the order and passed it through the opening to the kitchen, where evidently Mike the hash brown specialist was waiting. Grant tried not to let her expression—something close to a smirk but with a lot more challenge to it—get under his skin.

People didn't get under his skin. Certainly not in the space of minutes the way she had. People mostly annoyed him. Then again, people didn't send his mom home with a litter of puppies that she didn't need and shouldn't have.

After a few seconds, Grant came to the disturbing realization that he'd been staring. He couldn't figure out where that glow-y thing was coming from. As if Meg Kittering was sunny enough to cast the shadow for her own Sundial Diner. Even the space—all homey, with curtains and flowers on every table—glowed as if it generated its own sunshine.

He was annoying her—that much was clear—but the annoyance never fully filled her expression. Grant was used to reading people, sizing them and their motives up quickly so as to know how to respond. Her? Not so much.

"So," she said with an amused, nearly con-descending grin, "what's so terribly important back down in Billings—it is Billings, isn't it?—that you have to rush on back?"

Most people knew not to ask Grant about his work. Even Mom knew better. Partly because he didn't like to talk about it, and partly because most of it he couldn't talk about. Mom had no idea this spur-of-the-moment visit wasn't his idea, and he certainly wasn't going to tell her.

He wasn't going to tell Meg, either. Being told to "take some time off and get your head to-gether" wasn't the kind of thing you just brought up casually over breakfast. When he'd told Ser-geant Atkins he suspected there was deeply rooted corruption in the department, Grant ex-pected to be taken seriously. He did not expect to be told he was wrong and to ignore his suspi-cions. He knew he was right, and he was pretty sure Atkins knew it as well. It was why the ser-geant's dismissal of his accusations made him so angry. To be sent away like some misbehav-ing schoolchild? Why was anyone surprised he'd punched a hole in the sergeant's wall?

"Work stuff," he answered, with enough of an edge to broadcast the topic was off-limits.

She was undaunted. "Police work, right?"

He didn't know how to respond to her fascina-tion with him. As if he were some complicated puzzle to be solved instead of a man just trying to untangle his current situation. There had to be a way to talk some quick sense into his mother and then get back to Billings to talk some sense into Atkins. "How about you just let me eat my breakfast in peace and quiet?"

Now she looked annoyed. He felt bad, but not bad enough to get chatty.

Meg glared at him with an exasperated glare that should not look that good on a woman. "Well, mister," she countered, "if you're looking for peace and quiet, you're in the wrong diner."

At this point, Grant was certain he was in the wrong town.

Chapter Two

"Can we go see the new puppies after school?" Sadie begged—again—as she tugged on Meg's arm the next morning. Herding her two daughters out the door proved a challenge, mostly because Tabitha and Sadie knew Friday was the one morning Meg did not have to go into the diner. Even so, that didn't mean she had unlimited time to get the girls where they needed to be.

Meg handed Sadie her backpack. "We're late. We'll talk about it later."

Sadie's lower lip jutted out. "I don't wanna talk about it later. I wanna know now."

I used to think your persistence was a virtue, Andy, she bemoaned to her late husband's memory. *Now that your girls have it, I'm not so sure.*

"Tomorrow is Saturday. I'm done at the diner early. I'll ask Miss Cay if we can go visit the puppies then."

Tabitha, the younger of the sisters at five, joined in the pout. "That's a whole day away."

Meg grabbed Tabitha's backpack and headed for the door. "I'm sure you'll survive."

She was normally fond of these morning walks. High Mountain was a beautiful town settled in the rural foothills of Montana. The walk reminded her of the charm her hometown possessed. The girls' chatter was so much more fun than the burden of worries that usually pulled Meg from sleep long before dawn. It was a short respite from her constant state of worry over money. Over scrambling to pay the next bill. And the one after that.

Halfway to Grace Community Church, where the girls' day care was housed, Sadie popped the question Meg was dreading. "Can we have one of the puppies? I've wanted a dog for forever."

"They're soooooo cute," Tabitha agreed. It was clear the girls had discussed this between themselves. Meg was about to be double-teamed.

The eight adorable puppies would tug on anyone's heart. But it was also clear they'd been neglected, and at least one of them seemed to have serious health problems. Grant wasn't totally off base in his worries; vet bills could be expensive, not to mention food and such. Meg knew she couldn't add one more thing to her life right now.

"They are cute," Meg offered. "But dogs are a lot of work. And puppies can't stay home alone. Who'd watch it when you're at school?" It was an uphill battle to get the girls to understand the responsibilities of a dog, but it was worth a try.

Sadie looked up at her with the same eyes Andy had used when persuading Meg to get in on his latest sure-thing investment deal. "It can come to the diner with you. Everybody loves puppies."

Everybody except the food-safety inspector, Meg thought. *And maybe Grant Emerson.* "Dogs aren't allowed in restaurants."

"Miss Cay could take care of it," suggested Tabitha.

Meg adjusted the bow on one of Tabitha's pig-tails. "Miss Cay is *already* taking care of the puppies. That's what she's always wanted to do. Besides, we live next door, so we can go visit them any time we want. It'd be almost like having one, right?"

Sadie wasn't buying the argument. "I wanna go visit them right now."

"It's early," Meg replied. "They're still asleep." She didn't know if that was true, but she also imagined it was early enough that Grant Emerson would likely still be in his pre-caffein-ated grump mode over there. Was it fair to say a prayer that he succeeded in his goal of keeping his trip short? That way he was less likely to talk Cay out of the rescue-farm idea, or into selling the land. In any case, grumpy Officer Emerson wasn't anyone she was eager to see again.

Sadie's tug pulled her from her thoughts. "So whatdaya think, Mom?"

"About what, honey?"

Sadie gave an eye roll that made Meg dread her daughter's teenage years. "About the name. Oscar is a great name for a dog, don't you think? When we get one of the puppies, I wanna name him Oscar."

Clearly her sensible argument against owning one of the puppies hadn't sunk in. At all. "I did *not* say we were getting one of the puppies, girls."

The resulting silence and dejected plodding of little white sneakers along the sidewalk dumped guilt onto Meg's already sinking shoulders. She'd had a dog growing up. She *did* want the girls to own a dog one day. Just not now. Now she was stretched so thin she could barely imagine owning a goldfish. All her focus needed to be on getting her financial house in order. Making the Sundial a solid business so she never missed another payment. Banks weren't forgiving on these kinds of things. The mortgage company didn't care that some days Meg dragged herself home from a day at the diner feeling as if her very soul was drained out of her.

Honestly, it was half the reason the farm next door had such a pull on her. It had so much space.

The rescue farm offered such generosity toward animals someone had abandoned. That kind of generosity was deep in her own nature, but it was feeling squashed by the not-enoughs of life. Not enough time. Not enough money. Not enough customers. Cay seemed to have so much to give to the world. What would it feel like to live that every day instead of just longing for it from across the field? *Promise me I'll get there one day, Lord.*

"Can you please-please-please ask Miss Cay if we can visit the puppies today *and* tomorrow?" Tabitha pleaded.

Inviting Cay to drop by for coffee felt like a nice idea. Certainly a better way to spend her morning than dealing with the never-ending pile of veterans benefits paperwork and bank loan notices she had waiting on her desk. Or wrestling with which of her several overdue bills to pay next. "Sure. I can do that. But if Miss Cay says not today, that means not today. Got it?"

"She'll say yes," Sadie said with certainty. "Miss Cay always says yes to everything."

They'd reached the day care center. "Good morning, Tabitha. Good morning, Sadie," called Mrs. Watkins, the head of the preschool and before-school care. "How are the Kittering girls today?"

"Sad we're not with the puppies," Sadie pronounced.

"I heard about Cay's puppies." The woman looked at Tabitha and Sadie. "How fun that you live right next door. You'll get to see lots of them."

"I want one," persisted Tabitha.

Meg shot Mrs. Watkins a *back me up here* look over the girls' heads.

Mrs. Watkins nodded and returned her gaze to the girls. "Oh, they're a lot of work. I'd want to let Miss Cay take that on while you can just go over and play with them."

"But it can't sleep with us that way," Sadie retorted. Clearly the girls had been giving this a great deal of thought. This was definitely going to be an uphill battle. The best thing to do might be to bring Cay in to support the idea that she wanted to keep the puppies at her farm and the girls could visit.

And then there was Grant, who might very well try to foist the entire litter onto anyone who wasn't his mother. He was likely on the phone to his cousin Vicky, asking her to fire up her veterinary contacts to adopt those puppies ASAP.

But in a contest of Grant versus Cay, Meg put her money on Cay.

"Aren't they just the sweetest things?" Mom cooed as the litter of puppies squirmed and whined and yipped in the playpen she'd had

Grant drag down from the attic and set up on the front porch.

They'd devoured the boiled chicken she had given them and were already looking hungry again. It made him wonder when the pups had eaten last before Mom scooped them up.

"Did you think they were so cute when they woke you up in the middle of the night?" More than once. In fact, Grant had heard bouts of whimpers dragging him awake so many times over the last two nights that he was seriously sleep deprived this morning.

Mom shot him one of her looks. "You act like I've never stayed up with a cranky baby before." Her eyes crinkled up just enough to let him know *which* cranky baby she was referring to. He and his gentle sister, Ivy, had always been polar opposites, even as kids.

He gave her a look right back. "That was thirty-two years ago." He knew better than to add, "You were younger then."

Mom picked up the smallest of the puppies, holding its dark nose close to her cheek and stroking the brown-and-white-spotted fur. "I'm worried about this one. Those back legs hardly seem to work at all."

Grant knew that would only double Mom's determination to make sure the little pup was okay. "Could be troublesome."

"It's nothing we can't handle. And Vicky said she'd help out with whatever we need." She sighed. "Besides, I think I might welcome a little trouble." She paused for a moment before adding, "It's been too quiet in this house. On this farm." Mom gazed up from the pup to stare across the wide acres of the Emerson family farm. The sun was casting the surrounding mountains in a golden glow that reminded him of Meg at the diner and the golden curls that framed her face.

He shook off the unbidden image. "Quiet's good." That was almost a joke coming from him, seeing how he'd left the farm to join the City of Billings Police Department as soon as he was able. He needed to get back there as soon as he was able, too. Every day he spent on this forced vacation was another day the corruption he'd uncovered dug itself deeper into the department. He needed to get Mom on the right track ASAP so he could return.

His mother's expression didn't give him much confidence on that front. She looked wistful as she stroked the puppy. "Your father's been gone five years. Your grandfather went to glory six months ago. I need to feel alive again, like I'm here to do something important."

Her somber talk worried him. Her sunshine had often kept him going in a world where far too much was wrong. Had he ever told her that? Should he?

He knew she'd grieved Grandpa's long, slow demise—how could she not?—but it dug under his skin to hear her admit to sadness. He needed to get back to Billings, but he kept seeing reasons not to be in such a hurry to leave. If he stayed a bit longer, could he succeed in convincing her this large hunk of land and this big house were too much to handle on her own?

"We're going to call it Three Sisters Rescue Farm."

Her declaration told Grant he had a challenge on his hands. "These little darlings are a great start," she went on, "but we'll take in any animal that comes to us, that God sends our way."

Grant felt his stomach tighten the way it always did when sensing danger. *She's in over her head. They all are.* Even with Aunt Peggy and Aunt Barb—the sisters of Three Sisters Rescue Farm—joining in, he didn't see how the three of them would have the resources to keep the place up. The attic doorknob had come off in his hand when he went up into those dusty eaves to fetch the ratty old playpen. The house was badly in need of repainting. He'd counted seven repairs that needed to be done in the couple of days he'd been here. And to add a bunch of unknown animals to that? He hadn't even been out to the barn or any of the other outbuildings yet, but it didn't take much imagination to know he'd find just as many problems there.

Even Mom had to admit the farm was getting away from her, and that could only last so long. It would be hard to face the minefield he had to walk back into at Billings while he had to worry about her here. It was too possible that the farm would get even further rundown—eventually— and that would slow down Mom and her sisters' opportunities to sell. He had to try to convince her to sell. Surely Gramps had left his daughters the farm so the sale would enable them to live out their senior years comfortably, not to launch a haphazard, lost-cause zoo.

"I'm going to be smart about this," Mom proclaimed as if she'd heard his thoughts. "Vicky's coming this afternoon to check them all out. Especially this little girl." She snuggled the runt a little closer. The pup looked up at her with grateful eyes, and Grant began to feel that fighting Three Sisters Rescue Farm would be like fighting gravity.

"I really don't think you should keep these puppies. Vicky can find homes for them."

She ignored his comment. "Well, you didn't come all the way up here to tell me that. We found the puppies *after* you arrived. And don't tell me you came to try and talk me into selling."

"You *should* sell, Mom."

"That's what you think, son. And you could have told me that on the phone. You *have* told me that on the phone. Quite a few times, in fact."

"Maybe I thought you needed to hear it in person." That was true, but it was only half the truth.

Mom pinned him with a look. "I'm not saying I'm not glad to see you. But I've been your mother long enough to know something else is going on. What aren't you telling me?"

That was yet another reason to keep this visit short. If he stayed, she'd eventually get the truth out of him. The dirty cops he'd uncovered. The corruption he was trying—and not succeeding—to expose. She shouldn't know now, and probably not ever. The fewer people who knew the details, the safer everyone was.

Grant was just struggling for some way to answer her when he was saved by the phone ringing. Mom deposited the puppy into his hands without warning. "Here, hold her while I go answer that."

The puppy squirmed and yipped at the sudden transfer. The wiggling ball of legs, ears and huge eyes seemed even smaller in his large hands. The back legs didn't seem to hold her weight. What other problems did the dogs have? Where was their mother? Mom had said Meg found the puppies dumped out behind the diner. Who'd do something like that? Why? His police instincts began picking apart the situation as if it were a crime.

"Oh, no, dear," he heard Mom say into the phone after a short pause. "I don't want to trouble you serving me when you serve other people all day long. You just come right over here, Meg. I've already made a vat of coffee for Grant, and we can all drink it on the porch while the puppies play."

Meg was coming over. Grant couldn't quite work out how he felt about seeing her again.

Chapter Three

❧

"Your coffee's almost as good as mine," Meg teased when Grant's mother had a steaming cup waiting even before Meg crossed the field between their houses.

"I like yours better," Mom replied as she handed her the mug. "Mostly because I don't have to make it."

The puppies began nudging each other around the playpen like a litter of brown, black and white bumper cars, rolling and tumbling with yips and whimpers. How could those little sounds carry so far in the house all night long?

Mom's chuckle at the pint-size chaos ended in a yawn. "Although Grant made the coffee this morning."

"Needed it," he admitted.

Meg smiled as she reached down into the playpen. At the appearance of her hand, the pups stopped carousing with each other and turned all at once to scramble toward her. They poked their small black noses into her hand as if she was hiding treats in her palm. "Little darlings keep you up last night, Cay?"

"A bit," Mom replied.

"A lot," Grant corrected.

Meg and Mom both shot him looks. As if he was somehow defective because he didn't find the creatures adorable enough to overcome all the chaos they caused. There were eight of them, for crying out loud. Grant began to feel outnumbered, but not enough to retreat back into the house.

"Meg lives right next door," Mom explained, pointing to the little house on the west edge of the property. "I can just imagine your little girls spending time over here when we've got all sorts of animals."

"You don't have to imagine. I could barely get them off to school this morning without a solemn promise to come over and play with the puppies this afternoon." Meg offered an apologetic smirk to Mom as she leaned back into the porch chair's cheery cushions. "You're going to be seeing a lot of me and the girls."

So she had little girls. Mom, who seemed to be expressly built to be a grandmother but hadn't gotten the chance from him or his sister, beamed at the mention of Meg's daughters.

"Tabitha and Sadie are welcome any time. You, too." She put a hand on the woman's arm. "You look weary, hon. Everything okay?"

There it was. A flicker of alarm behind Meg's eyes. He had enough experience with people in crisis to see when someone was feeling exposed. Worried you saw something they didn't want you to see. She covered it up almost instantly, but that didn't change what he'd seen.

"Just tired." Meg took a deep drink of coffee. Maybe for the hot, strong brew he'd made, but just as likely to buy her some time to cover. "The girls gave me a time of it this morning."

Mom slanted a glance his way. "Children can do that. Grant here was a veritable bear in the mornings. Still is."

"Oh, I've seen his prebreakfast charm," Meg replied with that teasing grin he didn't want to find so appealing. "He's nicer after you feed him."

Mom laughed. "Aren't we all?"

"How long have you lived next door?" Grant asked, to redirect the conversation from his morning manners—or lack thereof.

"We bought the place two years before my husband passed. It was a stretch beyond our budget, but the setting is just so lovely we couldn't resist."

Grant watched something else flash behind her eyes. Grief, yes, but something closer to worry as well. The house was small and basic, half the size of the big white farmhouse Mom occupied. Things must have been pretty tight for Meg and her husband if that small house was a stretch. Maybe they were still tight. After all, it had to be rough to make it on your own with two small girls. And the diner had to be hard work.

"I'm sorry for your loss," he said to her.

"Andy was an adventurer," Mom said. "One of those daring air force test pilots. A real hero."

He'd often heard the married guys on the force talk about how much they put their wives through. "Must've been a challenge to be married to someone like that."

"It wasn't...until it was. You deny what they do, because you can't really live with it day to day if you think about it too much. But it's who they are, and you learn to love that part of them, too. Until..." Her words trailed off.

"Andy was killed in a test-flight crash two years ago," Mom said softly.

That explained some of what he saw behind Meg's eyes. But it didn't explain all of it. Grant told himself he didn't need to know.

"Wait till you meet Tabitha and Sadie. Darlings, the pair of 'em. I wouldn't mind seeing more of those girls. Like I was telling Grant this morning, I've been needing more life on this farm."

Grant noticed one of the puppies nipping on another's ear. The resulting howl set the whole lot of them off. They had to sleep at *some* point, didn't they?

"Where are my manners?" Mom proclaimed above the din. "I've got cake and I haven't offered you any."

Mom's carrot cake was legendary, launching Grant's life-long appetite for good cake. He wouldn't admit to sneaking a piece before Mom had come down for breakfast. Cake and strong coffee made an excellent start to the day.

Meg started to object, but Mom was gone before two words could be said. Meg stared after his mother as the screen door banged shut behind her, and they both could hear Mom singing as she made her way to the kitchen.

"No stopping her, is there?" Meg offered.

"Hoping that's not true." Grant was fully aware of the battle he was now waging. "Don't suppose I could interest you in a litter of puppies?"

She laughed outright at that. Even with the weary touches he saw in her eyes, it was a bright sound. "I have my hands full trying to make a go of the Sundial, thank you very much."

"Uphill climb?" he asked, just to see how she'd answer.

She didn't, and that said a lot.

Why had Grant asked if the Sundial was an uphill climb? Did Cay know something? She'd been so careful not to tell anyone about the tight finances, about missing the house payment. She didn't want anyone's pity. She *was* going to make a success of the Sundial Diner, and she *was* going to stay here in the tiny house next to Cay's farm. She certainly wasn't going to give Grant Emerson—or anyone else, for that matter—reason to think otherwise.

"You're going to need a bigger pen," she declared, just to break the tension of his nosy question. "This won't hold them for more than a day. Are you here long enough that you can build something? Maybe with some fencing from the supply store?"

Grant looked at her the way Tabitha did when told to do chores. "I don't want to do anything to encourage this."

He still thought he had a chance of stopping Cay. Meg still couldn't understand why he even thought he should. A total stranger might have doubts as to whether a woman like Cay should tackle such an ambitious project, but Grant had to know his mother's spirit. Surely he could see it for the virtue it was, not the liability he seemed to view it.

"I think it's wonderful. I love the idea. I'm looking forward to living next to Three Sisters Rescue Farm. And my girls are even happier about it than I am."

He looked at her as if she'd spoken in Latin. "You're not worried about what happens when this thing gets too big?" He pointed toward her house. "You're right over there."

"I'd much rather be next to this than to whatever development would come if she sells like you want her to. Honestly, Grant, you talk as if I'll wake up one morning to find a llama on my front porch," she teased.

"I just woke up to find these guys on mine."

Meg was used to speaking her mind. And giving advice, whether requested or not. She thought of it as part of the job of being behind the diner counter. "Maybe that's your problem right there. It's not *your* porch. Well, not anymore. It's *hers*." When he didn't bluster back a denial, she went a bit further. "You talk like Cay is an old lady. Fifty-eight is not old. She's got more energy than I do. This isn't beyond her. Besides, it's not just her working on this. She has Peggy and Barbara."

Grant frowned. "My aunts are just as likely to egg her on as to rein her in."

Meg had found Grant's grumpy disposition slightly endearing at first—like an Eeyore who hadn't found his Winnie the Pooh yet. Now it was starting to wear on her. He might be a very handsome man, with all that dark hair, broad shoulders and searing charcoal-gray eyes, but at the moment his spirit wasn't attractive at all. "Your mother does not need reining in."

There had been years where she had been just as fearless as Cay. And while she boasted a different kind of bravery than her test-pilot husband, she loved to tackle new things and challenges. Maybe that's why Grant's dismissal of his mother's dreams bothered her so—she never wanted to think of Tabitha or Sadie casting her in such a foolhardy light someday.

She wasn't foolhardy. She might be bearing the financial burden of Andy's foolhardy choices, but that was different. She could work her way out of this hole, and she would. It felt as if Cay's success would fuel her success, so Meg planned to support Cay in any way she could.

Meg lifted her chin. "I believe most people have great big possibilities. Look at her," she said, pointing to the limping runt of the litter. "Who knows what she's capable of?"

"Not walking well at the moment, for one."

She wasn't, certainly, but the little thing looked as if she desperately wanted to try. "Maybe she just needs some sort of procedure. Or one of those wheeled getups I've seen on TV." Tabitha and Sadie had been watching one of those veterinary shows the other week and dragged her into the living room to show her a beagle zipping around on the dog version of a wheelchair.

One of the boys in Sadie's class used crutches, and Meg was proud of how her girls treated him like every other classmate. She wouldn't be surprised if the girls made the suggestion when they visited this afternoon.

Weak legs could find help and support with all kinds of adaptations. Struggling moms could scratch and claw their way out of debt. Weak and sour spirits like Grant's? You couldn't solve that with gumption and gadgets.

"Sounds expensive," was all Grant could reply. It proved her point about his disposition, didn't it?

"There's our boy Grant!" came a melodic call from inside as the screen door opened to reveal both of Grant's aunts. Meg had been so focused on Grant and the puppies she hadn't heard the sisters come up the drive. This might be entertaining—the sisters shared Cay's personality, and would likely give their nephew a talking-to over the cold water he was dousing on their dream. And who on earth would dare to call the mountain of a man in front of her "our boy"?

The look on Grant's face told Meg he was having the same thought. She tried to hide her grin but failed. Meg could barely contain a giggle. The McNally sisters were among her favorite customers. She loved their optimism and unsinkable spirits—both things she'd sorely needed in her life lately.

Grant pulled himself upright from where he was hunched over the puppies. "Hello, Aunt Peggy, Aunt Barb." He bent down so each of the aunts could plant a kiss on his cheek.

"Look at you," cooed Barbara. "Are you eating right? Not scraping by on coffee and whatever it is you policemen eat?"

"Look at the size of him," Peggy said, tilting her head upward as if eyeing a skyscraper. "Whatever it is he's eating, it's enough, I'd say."

The next half an hour was a ruckus of yips, laughter, puppy snuggling and cake. Meg's heart felt ten times lighter than it had when she'd walked across the field. As an only child, she'd never shared the warm bond Cay did with her sisters. It was always in her prayers that Tabitha and Sadie grew up close and supportive of each other. That they would know a happy childhood in this charming house. *Help me save us*, she prayed as she gazed at the puppies Cay had saved. *Help me keep our heads above water and not miss another payment.* She would fight as hard as she could to keep from falling prey to her financial struggle, but some days it felt like a task only God's mighty hand could pull off. Some days she limped along as slow and cumbersome as the smallest puppy with the faulty back legs. No one could deny that little one needed help.

Asking for her own help—even though she

knew people like the McNally sisters would gladly give it—felt too much like a defeat. If it came to it, if it became the only way she could keep the house, she would. For the sake of the girls, if not for herself. *Don't let it come to that, Lord. Be my strength, be my courage, be my provider.*

"Come on, Grant, hold some of these sweeties." Peggy's teasing voice pulled Meg from her thoughts. "It'll be good for you," she said as she deposited two of the pups into Grant's lap despite his obvious reluctance.

"I've already held one," he objected even as he wrapped his large hands around the wiggling animals to keep them from slipping out of his lap.

"Well, now hold two. There's more than enough to go around." Peggy passed out puppies the way Cay had passed out cake. Everyone had one or two puppies to hold.

"Good." Cay handed around the bowl of chicken. "Now, make sure they eat without wolfing it down."

Meg watched Grant set the two puppies on his lap and dole out precise portions to each of them. They sat quietly, looking up at him as if he'd somehow managed to assert his authority over the dogs. He looked as if he commanded obedience, but Meg wondered if anyone else could see the small sliver of amusement crinkling the corner of his eyes. He was trying not to have fun helping the sweet little things, but the puppies were having none of it. When one of them pushed up onto his chest and licked his ear, something dangerously close to a laugh escaped from the man.

What do you know? Meg thought. *There just might be a nice guy somewhere under there.*

Chapter Four

Grant stared at the single-word text on his phone Saturday morning and growled.

Don't.

Cryptic by design to someone else, Grant knew the exact meaning sent by his partner, Luke Mullins, back in Billings: don't come back yet. He didn't know Luke's reasons for the warning, but he trusted them.

He'd told Luke his plan to tie things up here in High Mountain and make an appearance— approved or not—back at the station on Tuesday. Every day he let the information he had on those dirty cops go undiscovered was a chance for them to sink their roots deeper into the department. Or higher up into the ranks. For all the peace and tranquility of High Mountain, Grant felt as if there was a clock shouting in the back of his mind.

And now he had to sit tight. Grant was terrible

at just sitting tight. He couldn't just bide his time here as he waited for things to cool off enough for his early return. He needed to invent some way to occupy himself. He could make use of the extra time he'd been given to talk more sense into Mom. Or maybe he could use it to figure out what was behind the look of hidden panic he kept seeing in Meg Kittering's eyes.

Opting to meet two goals at once, Grant dialed his cousin Vicky and asked her to meet him at the Sundial. "Can you give me your take on all the equipment Mom is going to need? And the medical costs?"

He heard Vicky's laugh on the other end of the line as well as the giggle of her young son, Taylor. "Still trying to talk her out of this?"

He grunted. "Are you going to help me or not?"

"Buy me lunch, and we'll see."

By the time he drove down into town to the diner, Vicky and her baby boy were deep in animated conversation with two little girls who bore such a deep resemblance to Meg there was no question who they were.

"That's three times this week," Meg called cheerily from her spot beside the register. "You're turning into a regular." She pointed to a booth near the back. "Vicky and Taylor are over there with my girls." The girls' hair was light and curly in the way all little girls seem to have, and their bubbly personalities out-bub-bled—if that was a word—their mother's.

"Hi, Mr. Grant," they called out in unison, the older added, "We're showing Taylor about the puppies."

"And drawing 'em," added the younger one with a grin that was missing one front tooth.

Everyone was talking puppies, Grant realized. In truth, his mother and aunts seemed to have no other topic of conversation. He did his best to tamp down his frustration and walked over.

"Hey there, cuz," she greeted as she handed a small snack to the toddler in a high chair at the end of the table. "Good to see you in town."

"Only for a bit," he answered, hoping that was true. He'd need to find a way to talk to Luke and find out what had prompted the warning to keep away. Besides that, containing the pup-pies was becoming a real challenge. They'd es-caped their playpen yesterday and run all over the house. Mom found it amusing—until a pair of them started playing tug-of-war with her fa-vorite couch pillow, pulling the stuffing from two corners.

"We're making up puppy names," said the older one. "Miss Vicky's helping."

"Are you?" he quizzed his cousin as Taylor babbled his own reply.

"Want to hear some?" the younger girl asked before Vicky could answer.

"I like Fuzzy," said the older one, even though he'd not said he was interested in their name ideas. "And Licorice for the one who's mostly black. And Bernard."

The last one struck him as not your standard little-girl dog name. "Bernard?"

"Bernard's a good name for a dog, don't you think?"

The last Bernard Grant had encountered was a greasy, foul-mouthed man named Bernie he had yanked out from under a car as the man was trying to steal a catalytic converter. He had actually tried to bite him in an attempt to get away. Bernie was not a good name for a dog.

Meg saved him. "Tabitha, Sadie," she introduced, pointing to each of her daughters in turn, "Mr. Grant is having lunch with Dr. Vicky, okay?"

A thought struck him as Vicky set down her crayons. "How did you know I was Mr. Grant?" The girls had greeted him by name when he'd walked over.

"Easy," said Tabitha. "Mom said you were really, really big." So, Meg had been describing him to her daughters. He found himself hoping the description had a bit more depth than "really, really big." But in truth, had he given her much of anything more to go on?

Vicky chuckled. "Well, you *are* big. Kinda stand out in a crowd."

Sadie peered up at him as if he were a new puzzle someone had given her. "Can I ask you somethin'?"

"*May* I ask you *a question*," Meg corrected. She looked slightly embarrassed at the 'really, really big' remark. But also amused.

Again, Grant found himself wondering what other description she'd used. He didn't really need to care if he was only here for a few days, so why did he? "Sure," he agreed.

"Why don't you like the puppies? Everybody likes puppies."

Meg's cheeks went more pink, and the amused sparkle left her eyes. "Sadie!"

So, really, really big and doesn't like puppies, Grant thought. *Not exactly a glowing recommendation*. "I do like puppies," he refuted. "I had a dog when I was your age. I'm just worried that there are too many of them to take care of in the right way. Owning a dog is a lot of work. You have to be ready for the responsibility."

"Grannie Cay looks ready to me," Sadie replied, with an astounding amount of confidence for someone holding crayons.

"She luuuuvs the puppies," added Tabitha, as if that was all anyone needed to launch a rescue farm.

Grant raised an eyebrow at Meg. "Grannie Cay?"

"She *doppded* us," Tabitha explained, mispronouncing the word.

"She isn't a grannie to anyone else yet," Sadie added.

In truth, neither Grant nor his sister, Ivy, had managed to give Mom any hope of grandchildren yet. He had a theory that was half the reason the rescue-farm idea appealed to her so— Mom had a lot of love to give and not enough places to put it. That still didn't make it a reasonable idea.

"My parents live back East, and Andy's folks don't come around much since his passing," Meg explained. "I'm grateful for how Cay adores the girls." Again, that shadow passed over her eyes. There was much more to that story, he could tell. Not that he needed to know it, or had any right to, besides. If he had his way, he'd be back in Billings by the end of the week.

Vicky started to gather up her things to move to another table. "Aunt Cay is lucky to have you right next door. Puppies have lots of energy and need a lot of people to play with them." She looked tenderly at the toddler. "Just like you."

Grant made a mental note to ask Vicky how large the puppies would get. They didn't look to be small dogs, and dogs grew faster than little girls. An image came to mind of little Tabitha and Sadie amid a herd of large, rambunctious hounds. Or, for that matter, Mom amid a herd of them. Eight was definitely too many for one person. Controlling even a few could be a difficult task.

Couldn't Mom just start with getting one dog for herself? Did she have to keep them all? Forever?

"Now, you girls really do need to let Mr. Grant have his lunch with Dr. Vicky and Taylor," Meg said as she shooed Grant, Vicky and her baby toward an empty booth. "They're both very busy people, and the sitter is coming to take you and Taylor back to our house in half an hour." Both being widowed young moms, she and Vicky often shared a sitter to save on expenses. It helped Meg stay long enough at the diner to shave the extra waitstaff hours down to the bare minimum. She couldn't run the Sundial all on her own, but right now it was important to get as close to that as possible. She turned her attention to the adults. "I'll be by to take your order in a jiffy."

Meg took a deep breath as Grant, Vicky and Taylor shifted tables. She wasn't quite prepared for everything that had come out in that short conversation. Slipping in beside her girls, Meg gave Tabitha a stern look. "'Really, really big'?"

"That's what you said," Tabitha replied innocently. "And boy, is he ever. He's a giant."

"I did say that to you two. But it's not nice to point something like that out to someone."

"Doesn't he know he's big?" Sadie asked while chewing a bite of her sandwich.

Meg bit back a frustrated sigh. "What have I told you about talking with your mouth full? Of course Mr. Grant knows how big he is. It's just… well, it's not a nice thing to say."

She'd really hoped Grant would respond to the innocent comment with a laugh, but he hadn't. Grant didn't seem like the kind of man to laugh at much at all.

"But he asked," Tabitha persisted. "Wasn't I s'posed to tell the truth?"

Tabitha had her there. How many times had she said "Fine, just fine" to questions about how she was getting on? She had a meeting with her accountant later today, and she was fearful of what he'd say about her missed mortgage payment. Every day seemed to hand her a new reason to believe she wasn't handling life as a widowed mother well. The grief had subsided to a constant, dull sense of loss, but the overwhelm? The mountain of debt? That was still as vivid as the girls' drawings on the table in front of her.

Meg couldn't remember the last time she felt

anything close to abundance. Or true safety. Did the girls have enough? Did they notice the scraping by, the secondhand clothes and stretched meals? The concern that they picked up on her fears just made the fear worse—an endless, stomach-clenching spiral. Meg wanted to raise girls who believed anything was possible for them in this world. But how could a mother do that when she felt vulnerable and unprotected and on the edge of disaster every day? Maybe that was why Cay's great big generous dream appealed to her—Cay acted like there was always enough to go around and anything was possible. Meg yearned to be near that right now, and to *be* that someday.

"M-o-o-m-m!" Tabitha was tugging on her arm. "Wasn't I supposed to say that to Mr. Grant?"

Tabitha hadn't done anything wrong. A child shouldn't be made to feel bad for speaking the truth. And Grant *was* an enormous man, who hopefully heard about his size often enough that such a remark didn't bother him. He looked like nothing ever threatened him. If ever a man looked like a born protector, he did. She offered Tabitha a smile. "Grown-ups are hard to figure out, aren't they?"

"He grunts a lot," Tabitha assessed. "He's kinda Mr. Grunt, not Mr. Grant."

Meg leveled a glare at Tabitha meant to let her know just what she thought of that assessment. "You are never, *ever* to say that to him. Or anyone else. Now, finish up here while I take their orders, and then it's back home with the both of you and Taylor."

Meg made sure neither of the girls had any chance to see the grin that snuck across her face as she walked over to "Mr. Grunt" and Dr. Vicky's table to take their order.

Meg's accountant, Dave Peters, took off his glasses and pinched the bridge of his nose. "I'd hoped you would be posting more of a profit by now."

"I know." Meg offered an apologetic look to the only person in High Mountain who knew the size of the debt Andy had left her after his death. He'd been her accountant—her volunteer accountant because she couldn't afford to pay him in anything except free meals—long enough to earn the right to be brutally honest with her.

Dave shook his head. "Andy was a good friend, but he never did know when too far was too far. That man ate risk for breakfast."

And now she was paying the price. Literally. The pity in the look Dave gave her made her stomach twist. She hated pity. She hated having to admit to him she'd missed the last mortgage payment. Not even late; missed altogether. And it was going to be a stretch to make the next one, much less catch up. She couldn't bear the idea of anyone knowing how deep in debt her heroic husband had dug in his family in the name of the next great investment.

"I'm trying," she admitted, hoping it didn't sound like she was whining.

"You could lose the house, Meg. Your credit rating is hanging on by a thread as it is. Why won't you ask the church for help? Maybe access the food pantry."

She threw him a glare. "Imagine the owner of the local diner going to the food pantry. People will think I'm getting supplies to serve them at the Sundial." She took a steadying breath. "It's challenging, I admit. But I don't need help. I'll make it work. I have to. I just have to get out from underneath all this, and I will. Any good news on the Nevada land?"

Andy had fallen for some scheme one of his pilot buddies had concocted involving drilling land in Nevada. He'd never even asked Meg, just sunk too much money into the risky venture. It had, of course, failed. It seemed a horrible joke that the woman who yearned to one day own the farm next door owned a bunch of useless desert acres no one wanted to buy. If they could manage to sell it, the funds would go a long way to easing her money troubles. *If* they could manage to sell it.

"I've still got a guy trying to get that sold," Dave offered.

"Tell him to keep trying." Meg made herself ask the one question she shouldn't ask. "Dave," she began sheepishly, "we can't afford a dog, can we?"

Chapter Five

Late Monday afternoon, Grant stood back and assessed the pen he'd built inside the barn for the puppies. It hadn't been hard, seeing as how Vicky had told him exactly what was needed. Grant liked problems with easy solutions—his life just rarely offered them up. The puppies seemed to like it, and the structure would contain their active play. At least until they got bigger. Then he'd probably have to come back and build Mom another bigger one.

The hammering, sawing and assembling was as good a place as any to put his mounting frustrations. He'd dared to text back Why? to Luke, hoping his partner would find some way to communicate just how precarious his situation might be back at the department. The lack of response troubled him to no end.

"I can't just sit here," he told one puppy who seemed entirely too interested in chewing on his shoelace. "It just gets worse while I'm gone." And maybe that was the point of his exile, as he'd begun to call it in his mind. A clever plan to keep him out of the way and unable to raise any alarms while the dirty cops covered their tracks. It certainly was no vacation. Still, he trusted Luke's warning because he trusted Luke with his life. They were partners.

A noise from behind him pulled him from his thoughts, and he turned to find Meg framed in the sunshine of the barn door.

"Where are the girls?" he surprised himself by asking.

"Oh, I imagine they'll be here the minute after-school care lets out. Another mom walks them home some days, and I get a whole twenty minutes to myself." She spread her arms and grinned. He liked her grin. It was honest and sunny—things Grant didn't often see in his world.

"And you're spending it *here*?" The constant chaos of the puppies didn't seem like the best choice for a harried mom.

She shrugged. "They're fun to watch. And I owe you an apology."

His long legs stepped over the pen's fencing with ease. "What for?"

"Being called 'really, really big.'"

Grant smirked. "I am. Kind of an advantage in my line of work, anyway." He dared to clue her in that he'd overheard the girls' other remark. "And I have been told on occasion that I tend to grunt."

Her face went pale. "You heard that?"

"Cops are champion eavesdroppers." That was closer to a joke than most comments he made, but she had this odd way of pulling out the smallest bit of good humor he still had left.

They stood for moment, watching the tumble of paws and tails. "You are a bit of a grump, if you don't mind my saying. You seem...well...annoyed at being here. I don't get why. You're paying a visit to your mom. Seems like you two get along on *most* things." She emphasized the word *most*, nodding at his current position against the rescue farm. "And you said the day we met you were only staying the weekend. Why stay longer if you don't like it here?"

"I didn't say I don't like it here. This is my home." Was she always this nosy? "Am I not allowed to extend my time off?" It was a convenient half-truth. He was extending his originally planned stay, just not by choice. And yes, that annoyed him.

"Cay says you never take time off." She sat down on a hay bale, and Grant began to worry this wouldn't be a short conversation. "You certainly don't look like someone taking time off."

"Like I said, I'm checking up on Mom. And the farm." Also half-true.

"Diner owners are champion people-readers." She narrowed an eye at him. "This trip isn't just about your mom. Or the farm."

It made his skin itch to know she'd seen through his attempts to hide the frustration boiling up inside him. He was usually better at keeping things private. Given her expression and what he'd learned about her so far, it wasn't hard to guess she wouldn't let up. He'd need to tell her just enough to back off. Besides, it was far better to tell her than to tell Mom. "It's a work thing."

She waited for him to elaborate. When he didn't, she said, "Complicated?"

It was turning out to be a tangle of corruption and politics, but he wasn't going to tell her that. He'd skip the cause and just talk about the effect. "Alarmingly simple. Got called out for losing my temper one too many times."

She gave him a sideways glance. "For some reason I find that easy to believe. Was it for a good reason?"

No one ever asked him that. They always just got annoyed at him for losing his cool. "A very good reason."

"Want to tell me?" There she was, getting nosy again.

"No." He supposed she deserved that much honesty. The weird thing was, some strange, small corner of his chest actually *wanted* to tell her. Almost believed she'd understand. But no, he wasn't foolish enough to risk that.

He opted for a police tactic: go on the offensive. "Want to tell me why you're so stressed out?"

She flinched, then offered a too-quick laugh. "I'm the single mother of two small girls. Stressed out and exhausted is standard operating procedure."

While Grant could easily believe that was true, Vicky was also the single mom of a baby, and she didn't have the look of panic he occasionally glimpsed in Meg's eyes. "Nope. It's more than that." See, he could get nosy, too.

She pressed her lips together for a moment. "And how would you know that?"

"Cops have to be champion people-readers, too."

Another silence stretched between them, and he could almost feel her deciding whether or not to tell him.

"It's a money thing." She nearly whispered it, as if the barn walls had ears.

"A big money thing?" She had the house and the restaurant. Maybe that wasn't turning out to be enough.

Meg pulled her knees up on the hay bale and hugged them. It made her look small and fragile in a way that tugged at his protective nature.

"Really, really big," she said, echoing the girls' earlier words. "Gigantic."

He'd heard the girls use that word, too.

"Rough." He wasn't sure what else to say.

"Not my doing, but still my problem." He didn't believe her 'I'll make the best of it' tone.

It was easy to connect the dots. He'd seen too many stories like it. "Not to be disrespectful, but your late husband left you more than memories?" Mom had said Meg's husband had been some kind of hero test pilot killed in a crash. You'd think the military would take care of their own on something like that. Which probably meant a lot of money got spent where it shouldn't. And now here she was, trying to hold it together. Alone.

Her long, weary sigh said it all. "Wouldn't it be great if life was fair?"

It was such a Pollyanna question that Grant almost laughed. He couldn't quite bring himself to, though, on account of all the fear he saw in her eyes. "It isn't." He wasn't sure what compelled him to add, "I'm sorry," but he was. "Some people don't get the breaks they deserve."

"Oh, don't I know it." She stood up, brushed the straw off her pants with a soft little determination that almost made him smile. He caught the scent of her hair—clean and sunny—as she walked past him to climb into the pen with the puppies. "I suppose that's why I like these little guys. They had a bad start in life by no fault of their own. But they got their break. It's like God's reminder that good things still happen."

Grant didn't quite see it that way. Then again, Meg's face transformed as the gleeful pile-on of paws and ears and tongues and tails drew a laugh from her.

Maybe it did make sense that she spent her precious few spare minutes here.

He rather liked that she did.

"C'mon, you silly old door, give." Meg jostled the lock again Wednesday morning, failing to hear the click that told her the key had worked. The bolt hadn't thrown from the inside, so she'd come around to the sidewalk to see if she could move the sticky tumblers from the outside. "I can't open the diner if I can't *open* the diner."

"Breaking and entering?" came a voice from behind her.

She turned to find Grant with something close to amusement on his face. Well, what she expected amusement looked like on his serious features. Did the man ever truly smile?

"Lock's stuck." What had he said the other day about some people never catching a break? It sure felt like that this morning.

He held out his hand. "Want me to try?"

Meg didn't much care to ask for help, but Mike was running late, the diner needed to be open soon and there were no funds in this month's budget to call a locksmith. She pressed her lips into a tight smile and dropped the keys into his hand.

They looked tiny in his massive palm. He took a moment to peer at the pink plastic spatula keychain Sadie had given her for Christmas, then separated out the key she'd been using. "Stuck or slipping?"

"Stuck. The thing refuses to turn. And it worked perfectly fine yesterday." That wasn't exactly true. The front door lock had been becoming increasingly sticky for the past month. She'd been saying prayers the mechanism would hold out until next month, when she might be able to scrape together the funds for a new lock, but to no avail. Scarcity reared its bitter head everywhere she looked lately. She didn't like what that was doing to her spirit.

Grant examined the key, then bent down— nearly in half, it seemed, given how tall the man was—and squinted at the lock. He tried it, twice, but got the same results Meg had in her attempts.

Grant tried twice more, then handed the keys back to her and started to walk away.

"You're just going to leave me here?" she called, more sharply than she would have liked.

"No, I'm going to my truck to get a can of WD-40," he called back without turning around. "What kind of guy do you think I am?"

I'm still trying to figure that out, Meg thought.

Grant returned holding a blue can with what looked like a straw sticking out of it. "Oil." He squatted down to poke the straw into the keyhole. He squirted a healthy dose of the oil into the lock, then held his hand out over his shoulder. "Key."

Grant Emerson never seemed to use two words when one would do. Meg said a quick prayer for both her lock and her outlook as she gave the keys back to him.

He slid the key in, jiggled it back and forth a bit, and then threw the bolt to the delightful sound of the lock opening.

"Thank you!" Meg said, planting a hand on his shoulder while he was still crouched in front of the lock. "Thank you!" He was as solid as she expected. Lean and fit in the way Andy had always been, but so much bigger. Perhaps the lock realized what it was up against and had surrendered wisely. Or perhaps God simply answered her prayer for both the lock and the boost her sour spirit needed.

He jolted a bit at her touch, then rose up fast. If she was looking for evidence the man didn't like people to get too close, she'd found it. He'd stiffened a bit back in the barn when she had walked past him. But why? Cay Emerson was a champion hugger—all the sisters were. What made a man who grew up in that kind of family throw up such thick walls?

"Come on in. I owe you a cup of coffee at least, and breakfast is on the house if you've got the time." It would feel so good to be just a tiny bit generous—and it was far cheaper than a locksmith, anyways.

"You shouldn't be giving away meals."

She should have never told him about her money problems. "Don't you be telling me how to run my business, mister." It was mostly teasing. Mostly. She walked into the diner and finished snapping on the lights. Mike would be here in a few minutes, but she'd gladly make Grant breakfast herself.

"What'll it be? Eggs are fast, but pancakes stick with you longer."

"Eggs, sausage and hash browns," he said, repeating his order from the other day.

Meg measured grounds into the coffee machine, nodding as she added an extra half scoop. "'Cause I know you like it strong."

He nodded in return. "Appreciated. At least I'm getting decent sleep now that the puppies are in the barn."

Freely offered information she didn't have to

grill him for. That was a small improvement. "They're sleeping through the night?"

He frowned. "Mom gets up once to check on them. I've tried to stop her, even offered to go in her place, but you know Mom."

Meg tried to imagine a bleary-eyed Grant sitting in the barn pen, surrounded by puppies in the middle of the night. Cay? Yes. Grant? No. "Part of caretaking, I suppose." She gave Grant a direct look as she set the large empty coffee mug before him. "Your mom knows what she's getting into. You shouldn't worry so much."

The frown deepened. "Mom only *thinks* she knows what she's getting into. And what kind of son would I be if I didn't worry?"

He had her there.

"If it were your daughters launching a wild idea like this, wouldn't you be concerned?"

He had her there, too. "I want my daughters to be brave girls who…" She almost said "take risks," but those were dangerous words in her world. She finished with, "…aren't afraid to be generous and take leaps of faith." Meg felt convicted by her own words. She'd been growing more and more afraid of both those things in recent weeks.

"This rescue-farm thing is a mile-high parachute jump of faith," he revised.

Meg heard the sound of Mike coming in the

back door as the coffee machine started percolating. The diner began to fill with the sounds
of morning and the smells of breakfast. "But
there *is* faith. Your mom believes God's given
her this plan and that He sent those puppies to
kick things off. And I happen to agree with her."
When he didn't put up an instant resistance, Meg
tried a small leap of faith of her own. "I know
you grew up in a house of faith. Did you keep
it?"

His arched eyebrows showed how much the
direct question surprised him. "You mean, do I
still believe in God?" Grant thought for a moment before going further. "I believe He's there.
Let's just say we're not exactly on speaking
terms."

Oh, there very much was a story behind those
words. God was a constant presence in Cay's
life. In fact, each of the McNally sisters were
fierce in their faith. What pulls that out of a
man? Was it whatever his work thing was or
something earlier in his life? Or both?

She chose to tell him the truth, wanting to see
his reaction. "What would you say if I told you
that right before you came up, I was asking God
to send me some help with my door?"

He scowled. "I'm a passerby with a can of oil,
Meg, not an answer to prayer."

It was the first time he'd used her name. She

was making a tiny crack in Grant's thick wall of distance he'd put between himself and the world.

She smiled at him, enjoying a small glow of generosity at making this man breakfast in thanks for his help. "Well, mister, I just happen to think you can be both."

Chapter Six

Stay put.

Grant glared at the text his partner, Luke, had sent, this time from a number Grant didn't recognize. Which meant Luke had opted to use a burner phone after the text Grant had sent earlier. All this delay felt like the other side was winning, and it burned in his gut like an insult.

He did what he'd begun to do every time his current exile made him mad—he went to go fix something in the barn.

Only he wasn't going to get the solitude he'd hoped for—Mom and Meg and the girls were inside, trying to wrestle collars onto the dogs. At least he could take satisfaction in the fact that he'd built a good pen. A sturdy pen. One that would allow the puppies to get by without constant supervision. They were wearing Mom out, even if she refused to admit it. How many times had he caught her napping on the porch chair in the last six days? Did she really think he believed that "I'm just resting my eyes" nonsense?

"Look at them running around," Mom said as she called him over. "Girls and puppies—what could be sweeter?"

Grant noticed a pair of bandages on his mother's arm. "How'd you hurt yourself?"

She waved off his question. "Oh, I'm fine, you big worrywart." She probably wouldn't admit it to him if she wasn't. He was straining to view his ever-lengthening stay here as more time to convince Mom to be more sensible about this whole animal rescue thing.

He gave her a look and pointed to the bandages.

"I cut myself in the kitchen," she explained in an irritated voice. "Satisfied, Officer Nosy?" Her eyes strayed toward the little runt in the corner. "It's *her* we should be worried about." The smallest dog tried to keep up with the other dogs' antics, but it was clear her hind legs couldn't really support anything beyond a slow wobble.

Vicky had admitted worrying about that one as well. He'd asked her to chart out for him all the expenses involved in the puppies' veterinary care over the next six months. He'd done the same with the supply store for food, fencing and other needs. It wasn't a small figure, and proved what he'd suspected: Mom's overly optimistic estimates fell way short of what he thought all this would take.

"Sadie showed me a video the other day of a little puppy using a canine wheelchair," Meg said as Tabitha left off playing with the other puppies to go over and sit with the lame runt. "She declared she ought to have one of those. That we should buy it for her birthday."

That sounded like a very expensive gift for someone with money issues. "Dogs don't get birthday presents," Grant refuted. "Even if we did know the day they were born."

Mom turned to look at Grant. "I beg your pardon. I happen to know a little boy who made his dog a go-cart for his birthday. Pushed him down the hill in it. Poor thing squealed like a piglet and wouldn't go near the hill for days."

"You didn't," Meg gasped, clearly amused.

It wasn't as if he could lie now. "Bad idea. And not an argument for Tabitha's suggestion."

Vicky had, in fact, mentioned an expensive-sounding surgery to repair the dog's hind legs. The wheelchair-like device might be less expensive, but it was still a big bill. Would such a thing even work on the farm's bumpy ground and barn straw? Grant couldn't believe he was weighing such options. Still, he knew what Mom's position would be: do whatever was needed, no matter the cost. And while he admired her big heart, it was likely to drain her bank account.

"You know," Meg began, her tone careful, "the way you're thinking about running this place, you're going to see lots of animals with problems. There'll probably be reasons why the animals were abandoned. It could get expensive."

Finally! Grant shouted in his mind. Someone else was thinking about how much all this would cost, too. He hadn't expected backup to come from Meg, but he'd take it. And gladly.

"I've been thinking on that," Mom said. "It's just puppies now, but I doubt that little girl will be the last one to need some expensive treatment. And then there's all the food, more fencing and all the vet care."

"Definitely." Grant tried not to shout his agreement. Even Vicky's rough estimates made him nervous. Just taking on cats and dogs added up to some whopping figures. And Mom was making noise about taking in more unusual animals, like horses, those ridiculous miniature pigs, goats—even sheep and llamas. The place would look like someone scooped up Noah's ark and plunked it down in the middle of Montana if Mom got her wish.

"My sisters and I think we might need to do some fundraising. High Mountain folks care.

We need some generous souls to help. There have got to be some out there, don't you think?"

This was not the solution Grant wanted to hear. Nor did he like the look that came over Meg's face. It was great that Mom realized she needed additional support, but Grant was pretty sure Meg shouldn't be the one to be stepping up.

Mom looked at Meg. "The more kinds of animals we take in, the more expensive this gets. Do you think the church will let us host a spaghetti dinner or something?"

Grant could barely suppress the urge to walk over and stop what he knew Meg was going to say next.

She took Mom's hand. "You know, I think maybe the Sundial could help. In fact, I think the diner *ought* to help."

If Grant's jaw hadn't actually dropped, it felt as if it had.

"Oh, honey," Mom said. "I couldn't ask you to do that."

"You didn't ask me. I just offered. I need to do something wild and generous…"

No you don't, Grant warned her in his mind. *Gigantic money thing? Remember?*

"…and this feels like just the thing," Meg went on.

Mom seemed oblivious. "It's a wonderful idea."

"It wouldn't take much," Meg continued, despite the glare Grant sent her. "I'll talk my supplier into giving me a whole bunch of hot dogs at a big discount. We'll set a special dinner and charge ten dollars a dog. Proceeds go to Three Sisters Rescue Farm."

"We can call it 'Hot Dogs for Dogs,'" Tabitha chimed in.

Was this the same woman who'd just been admitting to him how stressed she was? How was this a solution to any of her problems? "Who'd pay ten dollars for a hot dog?" he balked, just because he wouldn't break Meg's confidence by declaring his real objection.

"Everyone," Mom insisted, then turned to Meg. "I think a charity hot dog dinner is a perfectly brilliant idea."

Tabitha and Sadie began to sing, "Hot dogs for dogs, we love hot dogs for dogs," to the puppies, who instantly joined in with howls and barks.

The moment he could, Grant found a way to pull Meg outside the barn and away from the others. "What are you doing?"

Her look told him he hadn't kept the edge out of his voice. "I'm helping your mom."

"You don't need to be the one helping Mom."

Her chin rose. "Actually, I do. I'm drowning in the feeling like I don't have enough of anything. I don't like the way I think lately. The only way I know to fight that is to remind myself that I *do* have enough. More than enough, actually. Gratitude. Generosity. That's how I fight my problems, Grant. I know it makes no sense to you, but it makes sense to me."

"I just…"

She held up a finger at him, shushing him as if he were a child. "Don't." With that, she walked back into the barn.

Don't. That word was his worst enemy lately. First Luke and now Meg.

Grant leaned back against the barn wall and stared at the sky. *Gratitude, huh?* He scrambled for something to be thankful for about this new wrinkle. Well, Mom *had* come around to the idea that she shouldn't be draining her own bank account to do this. If folks in High Mountain really were ready to get behind the animal rescue farm, Mom stood a better chance of being protected. And if Meg's fundraiser fell flat, it might wake Mom up to the idea that this farm might be more than she and her sisters could handle on their own.

It was a thin trio of items. This gratitude thing still made no sense to him. Hot Dogs for Dogs wasn't a real solution—in fact, Grant wasn't sure it was any kind of solution at all—but he'd have to take it.

If You really did send those dogs, Grant challenged God, *You better be ready to send the funds, too.*

* * *

"It's pink!" the girls squealed Saturday morning as if they'd just unwrapped a favorite Christmas present in the middle of April.

"Well," said Vicky as she finished pulling the contraption from the box, "the company did have two other color choices, but since they were donating…"

See? Meg told herself. *You start with generosity, and good things follow.* In truth, the dark press of scarcity had eased up in just the few days since Hot Dogs for Dogs was announced. And the diner had seen a small burst in business, too.

"Daisy gets a pink one!" Sadie declared with glee.

All the dogs had names now, thanks to a cooperative effort between Cay, the other two sisters and the girls. Each of them chose to name two dogs, with the final two naming choices going to Meg and Vicky each. Cay had tried to get Grant to name one, but he'd firmly declined. Meg thought about naming one of her choices Grant or Grumpy just to get under his skin, but she decided that was neither fair to man nor dog. As such, the litter consisted now of Fuzzy, Licorice, Bernard, Daisy, Oscar, Duffy, Tulip and Sam.

"It's *very* pink," Meg admitted. The puppy-size wheeled harness was so bubble-gum pink it looked more like a toy than a medical device. Cay had insisted the girls come over and see Daisy's new helper. "How does it work?" she asked.

Getting the puppies into collars the other day had been a mad scramble. She didn't see how it would be any easier to fit Daisy into the harness that held the wheels to her back haunches.

Vicky eyed Daisy, sizing her up before making some adjustments to the pink straps. "It's kind of like a cross between a wheelchair and a chariot. She'll probably find it a bit baffling at first. You may have to encourage her."

"We can do that," Tabitha assured the veterinarian.

"We can *all* do that," Cay said, adding a teasing nudge to Grant. His reaction to the oh-so-pink mechanism was downright amusing. As if he could appreciate the usefulness but couldn't get his head around the joyful color of the thing. For a split second Meg pictured Grant standing on the opposite end of the barn calling, "Here, Daisy, c'mere girl!" in whatever version of a cheering voice the man possessed. It almost made her laugh out loud.

"Get ready, Daisy. This is gonna be fun!" Tabitha cheered as Dr. Vicky let Daisy sniff the device. Daisy pawed at it, then tried to chew on one of the wheels.

"Don't eat it!" Sadie called.

"It's okay. Puppies explore things with their mouths. She can't hurt it. At least, I don't think she can."

"I'll show you how to take it on and off later. For now, let me get it on and adjusted." Dr. Vicky spoke softly to the pup as she eased Daisy's limp back legs onto a little harness, then strapped a larger harness to her stomach in front of her hip joints.

"What if she won't use it?" Grant asked from his perch on another hay bale. His question earned glares from both girls, who clearly didn't appreciate the pessimism.

"It's happened once or twice, but usually with an older dog who can't adapt. I figure once Daisy realizes she can run with this, there'll be no stopping her."

Meg, Cay and the girls watched in awe as Dr. Vicky finished the final adjustments and then stepped back. Daisy looked frightened, tamping from one front leg to the other on the straw but not moving forward.

"C'mon, girl, you can do it," coaxed Cay, moving a few feet away from Daisy and waving a piece of chicken.

"Go, Daisy, go!" called Sadie.

Daisy refused to move. In fact, she backed up a bit and became startled by the wheels' motion.

Everyone tried to coax Daisy into trying out the wheels, with no results. Meg's heart sank as she watched her daughters' faces fall.

"Grant, you're the only one who hasn't tried," Cay announced. "Call her."

"She's not going to come to me," Grant grumbled.

"We won't know that unless you try," Meg said. "Don't just leave the poor thing standing there when she could be running around like all the other pups."

After tossing her a look, Grant got down off the hay bale, hunched down at his end of the pen and called in the most unenthusiastic voice Meg had ever heard, "Here, Daisy. Here, girl."

To the astonishment of every female in the room—and likely the rest of the litter—Daisy looked at Grant, sniffed and then promptly took a few cautious steps.

"Call her again, son," Cay said, a bit of wonder in her voice. "She listens to you."

Grant looked as if this was the last compliment he wanted to be paid. Again, in the most deadpan of deliveries, he said, "Here, Daisy."

Daisy picked up speed until the little dog and her candy-colored wheels rolled across the pen at a happy trot.

"She likes you!" the girls called in glee. "Look at how she likes you!"

Daisy reached Grant, and, as if compelled against his own will, the man gave the pup a little pat on the head. "Good girl," he nearly muttered.

"Well, I'll be," Cay said beside Meg. "Didn't see that coming."

"Pick her up and turn her this way," Vicky called. "Let's see if we can get her to come back."

Grant's enormous hands picked Daisy up easily, turning her back toward everyone else and returning the dog to the straw.

Tabitha and Sadie practically fell over themselves in enthusiastic invitation to Daisy. "C'mon back," they called. "You can do it."

Daisy angled her head back as if to ask Grant's permission. "Go on," he said, just the smallest hint of encouragement seeping into his otherwise gruff voice. "Get rolling."

When Daisy tamped her legs again, looking uncertain, Grant gave her a little nudge. Then he stood up beside her and took one step ahead.

To Meg's astonishment, Daisy followed. "That's it, you got it." Grant took another step, and Daisy rolled forward a foot or two. When Grant crossed the pen in half a dozen easy strides, so did Daisy.

Vicky was clearly as amused as everyone else at the unlikely connection. "I think you made a new friend, cuz."

"Probably just smells the bacon grease I

spilled on my shoe," Grant offered. No one believed him.

"Make a slow arc and see if you can lure her into turning," Vicky suggested.

When he walked in a wide circle, Daisy followed. When he did so again in a tighter circle, she followed him again. Then, as if some little canine light bulb went off in her head, Daisy began turning and twisting and trotting around the pen with ease.

Cay took out her phone and began taking pictures. "I need to send these to Peggy and Barb. This is the sweetest thing I've seen in ages."

"She can run with all her brothers and sisters now," Sadie said, clapping her hands.

"Well, maybe soon, but just walking is a great start," Vicky advised.

Cay strode over and shut the barn door. "No time like the present. They can't get out of here. Let's let 'em loose and see what happens."

Meg wondered about the wisdom of that. There were endless nooks and corners for puppies to run and hide. But they hadn't been given a chance to really run yet, and it felt wrong to deny the puppies the opportunity to stretch their legs. Or, in one case, their wheels. Would Daisy run, given her new ability? She wanted her girls to see a victory like that. To see what the wheelchair company's generosity had made possible.

"You're sure?" Grant asked with one hand on the pen gate. Maybe Grant needed to see what generosity makes possible, too.

"What could go wrong?" Cay replied.

A lot, Meg thought, even though the prediction failed to wipe the smile from her face.

Within minutes the barn was a happy chaos of running puppies barking and tumbling in the straw. Daisy was tentative at first, but when Grant began trotting around the barn—he didn't need to break into a full run with those long legs of his—Daisy followed. Slowly at first, but within minutes Daisy was as fast as the rest of the litter.

Sadie and Tabitha jumped and ran and shouted with so much joy Meg thought her heart would burst. Grant finally sat down on a bench where Meg, Vicky and Cay were playing spectators to the happy tumult.

She dared a grinning glance at Grant. "Look what you did."

The man nearly rolled his eyes. "I didn't do anything."

Meg made a face worthy of Tabitha's fiercest pout. "You don't believe that for a second." The friction of their last exchange outside the barn was beginning to melt away.

He glanced at his mother, then leaned toward Meg as if to share something he didn't want

Cay to hear. "You're not going to give me some speech about this, are you?"

It was the closest she'd been to him. She was reminded again of his size, but also of the small glimpse of softness under the gruff shell he showed the world. He smelled of wood chips and something spicy...and not at all of bacon grease.

Meg met his gaze, startled to see flecks of gold and green in what had seemed to be steel gray eyes from a distance. She lifted her chin, emboldened by the side of Grant Daisy had revealed.

"Oh, I think Daisy did the talking for me," she declared. "You were a blessing to that little dog."

Grant did what Grant always did when he didn't want to admit something. He grunted.

Grunt and grouse all you want, mister, Meg thought to herself. *I can see that tiny spark of light.*

That was the thing about sparks, however. They either grew or sputtered out.

Chapter Seven

"Sit."

Grant pointed at Bernard and gave the command with all the authority he could muster. Contrary to Grant's personal experience with another less adorable Bernie, this Bernard was proving to be one of the smartest of the puppies.

Except "Sit" seemed to baffle the little guy despite all the techniques Grant had looked up on a dog-training website. Instead of sitting, Bernard ran around Grant's legs as if it was the best of games.

Grant squatted down to the dog's height, which only earned him a jump up against his chest and a lick on his chin. "Don't you want to show off to all your brothers and sisters?" These dogs were going to need some obedience training, or Mom was going to end up with a herd of misbehaving canines. "Sit," he repeated, pushing gently down on the dog's rear haunches. When that only produced Bernard squirming out of his grasp to run around more, Grant sat back on the grass and fought the urge to just release the leash and let Bernie run off to whatever his rebellion had waiting for him.

"I feel just like that some days," came a voice from behind him. He turned to see Meg watching him.

"How long have you been there?"

"Long enough to know you're not getting through to Bernard. At least, not that way."

Grant held up the piece of steak he'd been offering as incentive. "I thought treats were supposed to work." Somehow he just knew Meg had some secret parenting formula that worked on puppies and would show him up. He ought to mind, but he couldn't really muster up the resentment in her presence.

She walked closer to him. She was always in bright, sunny colors. Even out here in the Montana sunshine, she seemed to brighten everything around her. "Treats are a tricky business. You've got to wield them right."

"And I suppose you're going to show me how." Again, were this anyone else, he'd be annoyed. But this was Meg. That phrase ended up in his thoughts too often. She seemed to be the exception to everything, and that stumped him worse than Bernie's misbehavior.

Meg held out her hand for the bit of steak. Grant was careful in how he placed it into her palm. Not exactly meaning to touch her fingers, but not exactly disappointed when he did. So many things in his life were hard and sharp, and she was so soft. But strong, too—he knew that about her.

Grant had needed to tug on the leash to get Bernard to come to him, but Meg didn't even need it. "Come here, Bernie," she said, her voice warm and inviting. "Come here, boy."

Bernie stopped chewing on a nearby stick, his ears perking up at the invitation. Meg widened her eyes and leaned down a bit, waving the chunk of steak. "Want this? Looks tasty, doesn't it?" How did she do that? Her voice somehow promised the moon in that morsel of steak.

Bernie was no fool. He knew a good thing when he saw one. He walked over, cocking his little dog face to one side in curiosity. He tried to nip the steak out of Meg's hand, but she was too fast for him. "Oh, no," she chided. "You've got to earn this."

Slowly, she moved the treat up above Bernard's head, just out of reach of his wildly sniffing nose. With a gentle stroke, she guided Bernard's back haunches down while he was busy looking up at the steak. "Sit," she said as his backside moved toward the ground. "Good sit!" she praised. "Good boy, Bernie! Good sit!"

She gave him the treat, then proceeded to lavish praise on the little guy as if he'd just won the Nobel Prize in Puppy Sitting. All Grant's frustration dissolved in her happy gushing. Bernard ate it up, too, and then obeyed "Sit" four times more with the other pieces of dried beef Grant had stashed in his pocket.

He stared at her, amazed. "How do you do that?"

She laughed. "Well, I could tell you that it's a short hop from puppies to children, but I'm not sure you'd believe me. Mostly it's the 'flies with honey' thing. You make them want to do what you want them to do. But, in your defense, I doubt that works in your world."

"No, ma'am, my world works nothing like here in High Mountain." Some small part of him recognized that his instinct to come here had been a good one. He'd been telling himself he was here for Mom—and he was—but it was getting harder to ignore that he was also here for himself.

When the dogs, Meg and even the girls had become part of that, he couldn't say. The idea of sitting here in the sunshine, watching Meg pour a ridiculous amount of love and praise on a puppy, was a pretty nice one.

He allowed himself to ask a daring question, one that had been gnawing at him. "How do you stay so...happy?" He'd seen her tired, puzzled, illogically impulsive—come on, the fundraiser

with her finances in the shape they were in?—
but never far from happy.

That made her laugh again, and it reminded
him how much he liked the sound. "Oh, I'm not
happy all the time."

"You look it." He wasn't sure that was a safe
thing to say.

"I get angry. I just don't walk around broad-
casting it the way you do."

The gentle chiding should have bothered him,
except that it was true. "What do you get mad
about?" He suddenly truly wanted to know. He
wanted her to feel safe enough with him to speak
it out loud, whatever it was.

Meg pulled the puppy onto her lap, stroking its
back and ears as if she needed the comfort to answer his question. "I get mad at Andy. That he always had to take the next assignment, the riskiest
test flight, the one-in-a-million chance with everything. He pushed and pushed and pushed, convinced it would always work out. I think he even
had me convinced. And he was a hero. Decorated,
a wall full of honors and a chest full of medals."

Bernie snuggled up closer to her as if the dog
knew she needed it. Meg took in a deep breath,
and Grant could see her decide to speak the
truth. He instinctively knew she didn't do that
with just anyone, and he was pleased she did
with him. "And eventually the odds caught up

with him. They had to, didn't they?" Her voice caught. "It was all so…so…"

Grant gave her the gift of his understanding. "Unnecessary."

She lifted her gaze to him, eyes glistening with tears and that powerful sensation of being totally, honestly seen. "Yes."

He didn't have to know the details to sense the situation. Andy had taken risk after risk with his own life as a test pilot. Ignoring what the consequences might be for her and the girls, or maybe just finding it an acceptable trade-off. It was likely the same bone-deep compulsion that drove every guy in law enforcement—every first responder, for that matter. It was something inside you. Something you had to do, despite the high price.

"Unfair," he added, watching the word strike home. Not in a cruel way, but with the sharp edge of a deep truth. With, he hoped, the gentle tone she had used so well.

"That, too. I got a whole collection of words like that."

They sat in silence for a moment. Grant was glad to be there. Not frustrated at being still stuck in High Mountain or annoyed at the situation he couldn't seem to control. He was just glad to be here, to be an understanding ear for her.

"Thank you," she said softly. The two words held ten times the praise she'd given Bernie. "For asking. And listening. You can't say stuff like that to just anybody."

He wouldn't let her make light of the situation. "You can say stuff like that to me." He couldn't give someone like Meg much of anything, but he could offer that much.

She held his gaze, until Bernie found something fascinating in the grass and scrambled off her lap.

"Come back here," she coaxed gently. He was sure Bernie would ignore her, but to Grant's surprise, the pup turned and looked at her. "Sit," she said sweetly.

Bernie considered her for a moment, head again cocked to one side, then sat.

Yeah, Grant thought. *I'd do what she said if she looked at me like that, too.* The dog was even smarter than he gave him credit for.

With a very uncomfortable jolt, Grant remembered the next command in the dog-training video:

Stay.

Now there was something he wouldn't do— couldn't do—no matter how Meg or anyone else looked at him.

He couldn't stay.

Barbara McNally White never minced words about anything. Just after lunch on Thursday, the woman plunked herself down at a counter stool at the Sundial Diner and asked Meg, "What do you think of my nephew?"

Meg remembered her last conversation with Grant and willed her hand to continue mopping up a spill. "Grant?"

"Of course Grant. Who else would I mean?"

The pointedness of Barb's remark led Meg to worry she hadn't hid her fascination with Mr. Grump as well as she liked. People were noticing how much time they spent together. The girls had grilled her about him at supper last night, and that couldn't lead to anything good. She was not in search of a relationship now. And even if she was, he kept talking about how he needed to get back to Billings. Above all, someone with any sort of risky job was definitely off the menu.

Meg placed a mug in front of the woman and filled it with coffee. If nothing else, it bought her a moment to choose her next words. "You do have other nephews, Barb."

"I know that. But you know very well I'm talking about Grant."

Meg knew what Barb took in her coffee—she knew the coffee preferences for almost everyone in town by heart. Which meant she knew that Grant took his black and strong, in the largest possible mug. Not that she would share that information with Barb at the moment. Instead, she set the sugar and cream down in front of Barb and watched her dump a load of both into her steaming cup.

"He seems nice enough." What else was she supposed to say? She wasn't about to talk about the deep currents she saw in the man or the peculiar affinity she was coming to feel for him.

Barb wasn't falling for it. "That's a cop-out—no pun intended." Barb was always making poor jokes and laughing at herself. Meg hoped she'd be the kind of woman who didn't take herself too seriously when she reached the sisters' ages. "If there's anything Grant isn't, it's nice enough. How such a sourpuss of a guy is the son of Cay, I'll never know. He's always been a glass-half-empty sort, but it seems to be worse lately."

So she wasn't the only one who noticed. But she had a feeling she was the only one he'd talked to about it. "I suppose."

"Well, whatever it is, I'm glad he came to High Mountain for a bit. Just in the nick of time, too. Those puppies are a handful. Don't get me wrong—I'm glad they're here, but they do take a lot of work. I'm wondering if one of us will have to stay over at the farm for a while when Grant goes back to Billings."

"Maybe they'll settle in faster than you expect." Meg was glad to move the conversation off the topic of Grant. And to remember the temporary nature of the man's stay here in town.

"If farmers can pray for rain, we can pray for sleeping puppies." Barb didn't even need to look at the menu. "I'll have the tuna melt on wheat."

Meg wrote up the order and slid the slip back to Mike in the kitchen. "I'll have the girls put that in their nightly prayers, too. They love helping out with the pups in any way they can." She'd had a dream the other night of the girls, years into the future, helping her around the farm as strong, beautiful young women. In the wonderful way that dreams have permission to bend the laws of time, she hadn't aged a bit. Meg had woken up with a stronger urge to see Three Sisters Rescue Farm grow and thrive and perhaps someday come into her own hands. What a treasure that would be!

"It's better since Grant has built them a pen in the barn," Barb went on. "Cay was looking a little worn around the edges there for a bit while they were in the house. I was glad to see him helping out instead of listing reasons why we shouldn't do it."

"I think he's trying to protect his mom. And all of you. He worries you've taken on something too big."

Barb scowled. "He worries, period." Then her

face took on a conspiratorial grin. "With one very surprising exception."

Meg didn't like the look on Barb's face, nor the tone of her voice. "And what's that?"

"That man changes when he's around you."

Meg began wiping down a stack of laminated menus. "It's the puppies that do that." Knowing Barb's relentless nature, she let herself add, "And I think the girls charm him a bit. For some reason, they're amused by his grumpiness. Like he's Eeyore from *Winnie the Pooh* or Oscar the Grouch from *Sesame Street*." In fact, Tabitha and Sadie had asked if they could invite Grant to Friends Day at school—something that shocked her. Grant? Why not one of the delightful McNally sisters and their new puppies? Why Mr. Grump?

"Oh, I don't think so." Barb stirred her coffee. "I don't think you think so, either."

Meg couldn't help but glance around to ensure none of the diner's other customers had heard the remark. "Barb..."

Barb waved away her dismissal. "What would be so awful about that? You know what they say about opposites. He wasn't always such a dark cloud. Maybe it just takes the right ray of sunshine to lighten him up." She leaned in. "Maybe it's time for some happiness to come back into your life."

The words dug under Meg's weariness to squeeze at her heart. "I am happy." The declaration brought to mind Grant's question about how she always looked happy. Was she? Truly?

"I have the diner and the girls," Meg went on. "I have wonderful customers like you and Cay and Peggy, who look out for me—a bit too much."

"That's not what I mean and you know it," Barb replied. "I know full well what's not been in my life since Frank passed on." The woman had been widowed for several years—certainly longer than Meg had been without Andy. "Now I worry I'm too old to change even if I did find someone."

"You are *not* too old," Meg objected. "Far from it. You're not even old, period. And even if you were—" Meg waved her dishrag as if it were a fan and put on a southern accent "—I hear senior romance is all the rage these days."

Barb gave a big, bold laugh. Each of the sisters had full, hearty laughs you could recognize from across a crowded room. It made Meg wonder what Grant would sound like if he really, truly laughed. She didn't like how the thought proved Barb's point.

"You're a sweet thing," Barb replied. "And who knows? Maybe some handsome silver fox will come into the antique store one day and

sweep me off my feet." She took a sip of coffee. "But we're not supposed to be talking about
me." She paused for a moment before declaring,
"He likes you."

Meg felt her eyes widen. "How on earth would
you know?"

"Well, I admit, the man's not much of an open
book. But I've known him for a long time, and
the signs are there. You fascinate him. He doesn't
quite know what to do with that. You're gonna
have to help him."

Fascinate. It was funny how Barb had chosen
that word. Grant fascinated her. She seemed to
see everything going on under the surface with
him. And he seemed to sense all that was going
on under the surface with her. It was unnerv-
ing—and, well, fascinating—to feel as if both
their secrets were apparent to each other like
that. And yet she knew her secret was as safe
with him as his was with her. That made her feel
close—too close—to the man.

How had she, even for a moment, forgotten
how shamelessly the three sisters could meddle? Meg leaned her elbows onto the counter and
fixed Barb with a serious look. "Barb. Even if
there were a heap of fascination between us—
and there isn't—"

"I—"

Meg pressed on, "This is *not* a time where I

can think about that. The diner is just getting its head above water, and the girls need every drop of my attention. I'm happy to help out at the farm, and to host Hot Dogs for Dogs, but even that takes a lot of doing." In truth, the diner did *not* have its head above water. She was dangerously close to not making the next mortgage payment. The bills still shouted at her from the locked drawer in her desk every night after the girls were asleep. Happy? She was very skilled at *looking* happy while inwardly being terrified.

Barb's face softened. "Maybe all of that would be easier if you weren't alone."

Alone. It wasn't fair how that word sank into her. Barb wasn't wrong about how things would be easier with a life partner again. But Grant was not the answer. She didn't see any way he could be.

It was time to address the deeper issue she had with the man. Nothing else might tamp down the matchmaking urges lighting sparks in Barb's eyes this afternoon.

"I'm not saying that's not true. But I could never—and I mean never, *ever*—get involved again with someone who takes that sort of risk. I can't spend one more second wondering if someone is going to come home. Andy wrung it all out of me." Meg's throat tightened, but she made herself continue. "The girls have lost so much.

I won't put them through it again." When the tears threatened to surface, she forced a weak laugh. "The perfect Prince Charming could walk through that door with four dozen roses, and I'd still say no."

Barb put a tender hand on Meg's arm. But after a second, a small smile turned up one corner of the woman's mouth, and she said, "But it seems to me that sometimes Prince Charming shows up when you'd least expect him."

Chapter Eight

You had to give the little pup credit. Despite her small size and the crazy contraption, Daisy was undaunted. She was a tiny canine version of Mom, defying common sense and all the odds. As Grant watched the puppies race around the barn Thursday afternoon, he couldn't help but admit how Daisy was now nearly as fast as speedy Sam. And nearly as fast into trouble.

Tabitha and Sadie yelped as Daisy once again took a turn too fast and jackknifed like a tiny, furry truck. Grant found himself hurrying over to help the puppy just as fast as Sadie and Tabitha did.

"Is she okay? Did she hurt herself?" Tabitha asked frantically as Daisy scrambled in the straw to upright herself.

Daisy's weak hind legs made it a difficult task. "Whoa there, little girl," Grant said as he tilted the pup back up onto her wheels and settled her hind legs back into position. "Your wheels aren't made for stunts like that."

His new position low on the ground sent the other puppies running over, and soon Grant found himself overrun with more paws, ears, tongues and noses. The girls as well, erupting in giggles until the whole thing felt like one tangle of silliness.

"They're jealous of Daisy," Sadie said between bouts of laughter as one puppy licked her ear gleefully.

Grant would never admit to the hint of envy he felt at the girls' easy joy. Mom insisted there were years where he was like that—young and silly and full of giggles—but he couldn't remember them.

"I like her best," Tabitha admitted. "She's special."

The dog with poorly functioning back legs wasn't weak or deformed; she was special. When had he lost the ability to look at the world like that? To see life as light and full of hope instead of dark, broken and corrupt?

"She likes you best," Sadie said as Daisy tried over and over to pull herself up onto Grant's legs so she could reach his chest and poke her nose into his neck and chin the way the other dogs were doing to the sisters. "Let her get up and lick you."

Grant was in no hurry to let Daisy use him like a bumpy on-ramp. Nor to have his ears and neck licked. His one mistake was to look to Meg for support, who sat a few feet away. Meg seemed utterly amused and in no hurry whatsoever to help him fend off the adorable assault. "She just wants to thank you for helping her," Meg teased.

"Let her thank you," Tabitha and Sadie chimed in.

"I don't need her thanks," he said as Daisy tried again to scramble up the leg of his jeans. There was no way the wheels would allow her up, but she didn't seem to care.

Sadie offered a pout. "That's not how it works. People need to say thanks. It's important." She pronounced the words with so much pint-size authority that Grant almost laughed.

"Is that so?" he said instead.

"Yup," Tabitha confirmed. "Mom says." Now the formal wording made sense. Grant could just hear Meg giving a speech of that sort to her daughters.

Sadie crawled over and put a hand on Grant's shoulder. "You're gonna have to lie down. She can't reach otherwise."

Grant cringed at the thought of the tiny pink tongue lapping at his face and ears. Or tiny pawprints on his shirt.

A moment later, Tabitha's hands were planted on his other shoulder, and the two of them began pushing him over. Grant had barely enough time to hoist Daisy and her wheels up onto his lap before he was flat on his back in the straw.

The girls squealed on each side of him, and he heard the delightful sound of Meg's laughter as Daisy made her wobbly way up his chest. She looked at him with her tiny head cocked to one side, as if to say, "How'd I get above you?"

"Hold still," came Tabitha's voice, one hand still clamped on his shoulder as if she had any hope of holding a man of his size down.

"Hard with all of you on me," he countered, earning more laughter from Meg. Of course she was enjoying this. What could be more fun that watching a grown man flattened by puppies and two girls who barely came up to his waist?

Daisy chose that moment to push her nose into his ear and sniff with such force that he burst out laughing. Not a small laugh, either. What Mom would have called a guffaw if she was here—and he was beyond thankful she was not.

The sound sent the girls into peals of laughter and the puppies barking. Above it all, Grant could pick out the sound of Meg's laugh. Something warm and wonderful broke open in his chest, and he lay back, unresisting, and let it happen.

Joy. It was the only word that came to mind. A word that hadn't come anywhere near his life in years. From the most unlikely place he could ever imagine.

"Okay, okay, I'm thanked already," he managed to gasp out after a few minutes. By this time, each of the girls was flat on her back with a puppy on her chest as well. Grant managed to prop himself up on both elbows, gaze level with Daisy's big brown eyes. "Done?" he asked.

Daisy's response was to settle against his chest, wheels still on his stomach, and lay her nose right over his heart. She gave a big sigh as if she'd drop off to sleep right there on top of him.

"That was so fun!" Tabitha said.

He turned to look at her. She had straw in her hair and smudges on her shirt. One shoe was off, and she had two puppies draped across her, each licking and nipping whatever they could reach. She looked exactly like the picture that should be in the dictionary next to the word *adorable*.

"You know," he found himself saying, "it really was."

"Your laugh isn't grumpy at all," Sadie said. "But it's really big."

Grant had never thought of himself as being in possession of a really big laugh. But he was a really big man, so it made sense. It was just that life hadn't handed him reasons to find out how big his laugh really was.

"Thank you," he said, genuinely meaning it.

"After all, it's important that people get to say thanks, isn't it?"

Grant looked up to catch Meg's gaze, and the warm sensation in his chest cracked open a bit more. He felt different around her, he admitted to himself. Around all of them. He knew what it was to be attracted to a woman, to admire her smile or curves or wit, but this felt altogether different.

And unreachable. As if the whole reason she appealed to him was bound up in the fact that he didn't belong anywhere near her. He could scramble as much as Daisy to get closer to her, but it wouldn't matter.

For one thing, he had nothing to offer her. Nothing that she needed, anyway. And for another, he knew, without her ever having to say it, that she'd never let him close.

None of that changed the long moment that they looked at each other. There was a glimmer of possibility, a warmth as pure as the laughter they'd just shared, but it wasn't a lasting kind.

He'd just have to take this glimmer of a moment and tuck it away. Pack it up with gratitude rather than envy or loss.

After all, it was important for people to say thanks. Right?

Their time with the puppies was all the girls could talk about that evening. They drew pictures. They recounted every detail. They dreamed up new challenges and antics for Daisy and her littermates.

And they talked about Grant. There had been a lot of talking about that man and his surprising burst of laughter. Thanks to the strength of the High Mountain community, the girls had several strong and compassionate men in their lives. Mike the cook was practically an uncle to them, and Pastor Jim went out of his way to be active in Tabitha's and Sadie's lives.

She didn't know what to make of this surprising reaction the girls had to Grant. He wasn't especially friendly, but they seemed to find it amusing rather than off-putting. He never spoke down to them—she had to give him that. Grant seemed to have some pint-size dose of respect for each of them as individual personalities. It was clear they baffled him, but that only seemed to egg the girls on.

"He laughs like a tuba," Tabitha said as Meg set out the plates for dinner. Her class had been studying orchestral instruments this week. "It's like big fat bubbles."

Meg chuckled at the inventive description. "I guess he does. He is a big man, after all." Tabitha had always been the most perceptive one, so Meg dared to ask, "Why do you think Daisy likes him so much?"

Tabitha, who was drawing a picture of Daisy, stopped coloring to consider her answer. "He has parts that don't work just like she does."

Grant Emerson was a large, strong, very fit man. Meg couldn't think of a single physical shortcoming. He was, when she dared to admit it, handsome. Thick, glossy hair and chiseled features, a broad chest and shoulders that looked like he could perch Tabitha and Sadie on each of them and walk for miles. "Really?" she asked her daughter. "What parts of him don't work?"

Tabitha looked up at her as if the answer was obvious. "His smile is broken."

Out of the mouths of babes. Tabitha had offered the innocent truth Meg would have thought only adults could see. It made her worry for a moment how she could ever hope to hide all her concerns and sorrow from the girls.

Meg sat down in the empty chair at one end of the table. The chair where Andy had sat. She often made a deliberate choice to sit there so that the girls didn't always see it as the empty place where their father had been, but at this moment she simply sank into it, pressed down by the power of Tabitha's remark.

"It is, isn't it?" If only such very grown-up pains could be fixed with ingenious pink wheels. "Maybe Daisy thinks if she shares her wheels, he'll find some fix of his own?"

"He's not looking to be fixed," Sadie said. "He likes being grumpy."

"Nobody likes to be grumpy." Meg refolded the napkin at Sadie's place setting. "It's just sometimes it's really hard not to be when tough things happen. That's why it's always good to do whatever you can to cheer people up." Her words about Grant could too easily be applied to herself.

Tabitha returned to her drawing, now adding a stick man to the paper. Meg noticed she gave the man a frowny face. "The puppies cheer me up a lot. And they made Mr. Grant laugh. But he still didn't smile."

There was a difference, wasn't there? "Well, maybe that'll have to be our job." The secrets they shared gave her an urge to help Grant. For all his strength, he seemed a bit lost. The complicated work thing that had landed him here had shaken him off his foundation. And while he'd never come out and said it, she was sure his vacation wasn't voluntary. He'd been sent away. But why? "How should we go about fixing Mr. Grant's broken smile?"

Sadie, always ready with a goofy answer, offered, "We could draw him a new one. On his face, like the clowns in the circus."

The image made Meg laugh. She got up to continue fixing dinner. "Oh, I don't think that will work. Besides, a smile has to come from the inside."

"I think he needs to have Daisy as his own puppy," Tabitha declared. "I kinda wanted her, but I think Mr. Grant needs her more."

So often Meg would wonder if the girls' massive loss would damage their outlook on life. If the trauma of their father's sudden and dramatic death would steal their innocence and optimism. And then one of them would say something like this, and remind her of how sweet and strong a child's heart could be.

She walked over to Tabitha and placed a hand on her daughter's shoulder. "That's a very kind thing to say, sweetheart. And I know how much you like Daisy. But I don't think Mr. Grant is the kind of man who wants a dog."

"But he had fun with them. Why wouldn't he?"

This was a chance to talk to the girls about responsibility. "Visiting and playing with a dog are fun things. But owning a dog takes a lot of work. And time. Mr. Grant's job makes that hard."

Mr. Grant's job. Meg recalled the strong speech she'd given Barb about how she could never let such a high level of risk back into her life. Andy had loved risk—thrived on it—but after a while, she could no longer feel his exhilaration. Lately, all she felt was the weight of the debts. The fallout from failed schemes Andy was always sure would make them rich. Not to mention the need to be a hero that drove him to jump at each chance to test something newer, faster or higher.

"We could help," Tabitha offered. "We could visit his dog like we visit the dogs at Grannie Cay's now."

"Mr. Grant doesn't live here in High Mountain, honey. He's just visiting." And there was another reason to ignore the warm pull she felt around the man with the broken smile. High Mountain was her home. And, if God was kind, Three Sisters Farm might someday be her home as well. How lovely it would be to pass it down decades from now to the two sisters right in front of her. She loved the diner and how it connected her to people, but ever since Cay had raised the idea of the rescue farm, the Sundial Diner had secretly become the thing she did to get ready to own the farm one day.

Which was almost absurd, given that Meg had never mentioned this pie-in-the-sky dream to anyone, much less Cay Emerson herself.

"He seems happy here," said Sadie.

"That's silly. He isn't happy anywhere," countered Tabitha, now adding bold black hair to the drawing of Grant and his equally bold frown.

Sadie's chin rose. "He laughed with the puppies. That's happy, isn't it?"

"Only for a minute," Tabitha argued back. Then she straightened, getting an idea. "What if we bake him a cake? I'm always happy when I have cake."

"Ooo, me, too!" Sadie chimed in. "Chocolate cake. With chocolate frosting. Lots of it."

If the way to a man's heart was supposedly through his stomach, could it be the way to his smile as well? How would Grant react if she and the girls presented him a cake for no reason? Did he have a birthday coming up? Maybe she could have cake ready for dessert at the diner and just present him with a slice.

Meg looked at her two daughters, debating the happiness of a man they'd only recently met.

The idea had a surprising lure. What if he was capable of joy underneath that hard exterior? The way he treated the girls and the puppies certainly hinted that he was. If bringing that side of Grant out wasn't worth a cake, she didn't know what was. It would feel good to make him feel a tiny bit special...and maybe a tiny bit happy for a minute before he returned to whatever dark challenge awaited him in Billings.

Because sometimes, she thought, *a minute is all you get.*

Chapter Nine

Grant pulled his truck into the parking lot of a nondescript diner by a highway a good ways from High Mountain on Friday. He'd had the entire drive from the farm to wonder why Mullins had suddenly taken the risk of sending a text asking for a meeting.

Something was up. Something big.

And since Grant had no intentions of that something coming anywhere near High Mountain, he'd suggested this tiny roadside diner half-way between.

His partner was already seated in a booth, hands wrapped around a cup of coffee. True to every cop's second nature, Luke had chosen a seat with a clear view of the door. In all his years on the force, Grant had never known a police-man—or most military vets, for that matter—to sit with his back to an exit. It was what made eating at the Sundial such a struggle; Meg always insisted he eat near her at the counter. And because he liked being near her, he did. But it meant his back was to the diner door, and that always made the base of his neck prickle.

Some habits stuck with you forever.

Some company was worth a bout of prickly neck.

Grant's neck prickled for an entirely different reason at the look on Mullins's face. Whatever news his partner had, it wasn't *It's safe to come back now.*

"Miss me?" Luke joked.

"Every hour," Grant joked back, easing his large frame into the red vinyl bench on the near side of the booth. Back to the exit, he noted, and attempted to file it away so he could pay attention to whatever it was Mullins had come here to say. He nodded to the friendly-faced waitress who appeared with a mug and a coffeepot. She poured his, topped off Mullins's mug, and took their orders for a pair of sandwiches Grant wondered if they'd stay long enough to eat.

Mullins dumped more cream into his coffee. "Enjoying yourself?"

Mullins and Sergeant Akins were the only two people back in Billings who knew the real, mandated nature of Grant's vacation.

"Immensely," Grant lied. "My inner peace could knock you flat at a hundred yards."

Mullins groaned. "You wouldn't know inner peace if it had you in a chokehold. At least you look calmer. Not like you're walking around winding up to take a swing at the world."

Nothing about the situation he'd left in Billings had changed. It was looking like his plan to go back early and expose the corruption that had landed him out here would not come to fruition. That should have made him want to wind up and take a swing at the world.

Only it didn't. It took him a while to realize the slowly unwinding sensation under his ribs was, in fact, calm. Where had that come from? Grant tried to stifle the notion that it wasn't *where* it had come from, but *who* it had come from.

They made departmental small talk until the food arrived, ensuring they wouldn't be interrupted again for a stretch of time while Mullins said what he'd come to say. Grant noted his Reuben sandwich smelled good, but the coffee didn't come close to Meg's. It made him wonder if he'd measure all coffee from now on against the quality of the Sundial's.

Mullins finally got to the point. "Jig's up. Internal Affairs has been sniffing around."

"Good." Someone was finally taking all those minor irregularities seriously over there. Grant had gotten tired of raising red flags with Atkins only to have them dismissed or outright ignored. Finally, someone was listening. Some of that calm dissolved, replaced by a new urge to get back to Billings and push for things to come to light.

"Yeah, but they're being too careful."

"What do you mean?"

"They're being really cautious," Mullins continued. "This goes high up, Grant. I'm not even supposed to know they're sniffing around. I only overheard a conversation with the sarge because I happened to be in the right place at the wrong time. Sarge doesn't know I know, and I aim to keep it that way."

Good cops shouldn't have to watch their backs within their own departments. Still, everybody knew justice was only what police provided, not necessarily what they got themselves. Grant's current involuntary vacation was proof of that. "Mullins, what do you know?"

Luke literally scanned the near-empty diner and then lowered his voice. "I think they know you're involved. They know you're the one who blew the whistle on this. And they aim to make sure no one listens to you."

Grant never doubted his suspicions that several sergeants—and at least one captain—were on the take. He just couldn't prove any of it. These guys were so clever that it appeared completely random unless you looked really close. Grant couldn't decide if the confirmation made him feel better or worse. This was one situation where he would have much preferred to be wrong.

"Are you saying Internal Affairs might be *in* on this?" Internal Affairs was supposed to be the arm of justice for the department, not just more of the problem. If the corruption went far enough up to have the brass looking for ways to shut Grant up, things were worse than he thought.

"It goes high up. Like, *way* high up."

He should be shocked. Still, the kind of bribery he suspected would need to go nearly all the way to the top. Greedy fingers skimming through every department and multiple higher-ups. The whole thing was like a snowfall—each flake tiny and light, but when you piled it all up, it could cave in the roof of a house. The way out of this—if there was one—was going to be messy and ugly.

"I'm not sure it's a bad thing that you're all the way out here."

Luke was telling him to stay put. Which could mean only one thing. "So it is true. I'm not out here for my own rehabilitation." He wasn't even out here for his own protection. "I played right into Sarge's hands by giving him a reason to get me out of the picture for a few weeks." He'd always known his temper was a liability, just not quite on this level. Regret and frustration smoldered under his ribs. He could be back there doing something about it if he hadn't lost it in front of Sarge.

The idea that Sarge was likely part of the whole thing stole any appetite Grant may have had. Here he'd been thinking he was doing the right thing by tipping Sarge off to a threat. No wonder the man had been so infuriatingly calm. Nothing Grant told him was news. Grant had simply outlined in perfect detail what he knew and the nature of the threat. He'd put every suspicion—every correct suspicion, it now seemed—on display for his sergeant. Revealing the crime to the culprit. Or one of many culprits.

Many well-placed, powerful, vengeful culprits.

Grant growled, only because it seemed like the better choice than all the low-life thoughts running through his brain at the moment. Was it any wonder Grant had punched a hole in the guy's wall? Was your temper really a problem if you were right?

"Look, you didn't hear this from me, okay?" Mullins said, looking more than a little worried. Grant recognized the risk Luke was taking in coming here and telling him this. It wasn't fair how everyone around him would be tainted by this. *Everyone around me...* His mind cast back to High Mountain and made his chest constrict.

"You gotta be careful, Luke," Grant warned. "Make sure they don't know you know. *Make sure*. No more meetings, and only text on the burner phone, and even then only if absolutely necessary. These guys don't play nice. They strike me as the kind who wouldn't think twice about hurting someone. Or worse." *Everyone around me...*

Mullins's face paled. "Are you thinking Rodale's accident maybe wasn't so accidental?" Arthur Rodale had been in a nasty car wreck two weeks before Grant's confrontation in the sergeant's office. A freak accident that seemed wildly out of place for one of the department's best drivers.

In fact, Rodale's unlikely accident was one of the clues Grant had brought up to his sergeant. "Could be."

Mullins pushed his plate away, his stomach evidently turning as Grant's had with the unwelcome news. "Now what?"

Grant drummed his fingers against his coffee mug. It was the thick, white ceramic kind, common in hundreds of diners. But it wasn't nearly big enough. He found himself wishing for the good brew in the great big mug Meg always saved for him.

"Not sure yet. Best thing we can do is sit tight and make like today never happened. If it doesn't go all the way up to Internal Affairs, they might be able to root it out. If it does, it'll take more than us to do anything about it."

Meg stared down the street Saturday afternoon, looking for Grant's truck. "Is he coming?"

Sadie went to the diner window and peered as well. "He has to."

"Well, that's exactly what I told him." Cay offered a *What else can I do?* expression to Meg. "He's been especially grumpy since yesterday."

Tabitha stood up the big green card the girls had made Grant. "Nobody gets to be grumpy on their birthday."

"I still can't believe it's actually his birthday today," Meg admitted. "I mean, we came up with the idea of cake without knowing anything."

Cay grinned. "I love when God shows off, don't you? Here I was, wondering how I could do something special for him, and then you call me asking if I can help you get Grant into the diner for a special cake."

"It was our idea," Sadie said, coming back from the window with a worried look on her face. "We thought it would fix his broken smile."

Meg worried Cay would take offense at the remark, but the woman gave Sadie the warmest of smiles. "It's a lovely idea, sweetheart. And that is a good way to put it. Grant's smile doesn't quite work lately, does it?"

"Why?" Tabitha asked, as if there were some simple explanation.

Of course, Meg knew the explanation was far from simple, even though she knew bits of it. She tried to think of some way to explain that didn't violate Grant's confidence, and ended up saying, "We don't know. But we don't have to know to help, do we?"

"I just know the cake'll help," Tabitha declared.

"We just have to get him here." Cay picked up her phone and texted her son for the second time. "All these people aren't going to wait around forever." Between the two of them, Cay and Meg had convinced the other customers to break into "Happy Birthday to You" when Grant walked through the door. Anticipating she'd need some leverage, Meg had baked an extra sheet cake to dole out to customers in addition to the large layer cake with a single candle in it, which sat under the glass dome on the counter.

"Oooh!" Cay cried as she tucked the phone back into her handbag. "There he is!"

If it was possible to see reluctance broadcast from the way a man got out of a vehicle, Grant looked to Meg as if he was dragging himself into the diner. He'd stayed away from the Sundial the last day or so, and had been distant when they met up at the farm. Something had happened, but she couldn't find a moment to ask.

The look of near horror that showed on his face as he walked through the door and the birthday chorus launched into song would have been funny had it not been so heartbreaking. The girls sang the loudest, and Meg said a small prayer that he'd consent to the celebration for their benefit, if nothing else. Despite everything that had happened to them, the girls had enormous hearts, and she didn't want to see that generous love squashed by whatever was weighing Grant down. Besides, the fact that their idea lined up with Grant's actual birthday gave her hope that God really had arranged it all.

"What's going on?" he said tightly, a dark look bouncing back and forth between herself and Cay.

Peggy and Barb stood up from the counter stools where they'd been waiting for their nephew. "Isn't it obvious?" Peggy asked. "We're celebrating your birthday."

Barb pointed to the counter where the cakes were waiting. "There's cake."

Grant stood still, feet planted only a handful of steps into the diner. "I didn't ask for cake."

Meg nearly held her breath as Tabitha walked up to Grant, totally undaunted by the man's sour reaction. "It was our idea. And then we found out it was your birthday. Isn't that amazing?"

Grant looked at Meg. "Boggles the mind." Then, as if his better nature suddenly found its way to the surface, Grant hunched down to Tabitha's height. "So you decided I ought to have a cake, huh?"

"Yep. Me and Sadie got the idea and Mom made the cake and Grannie Cay helped. It's chocolate. With chocolate frosting, too. Lots of it."

"Well, what do you know? Chocolate's my favorite."

The breath Meg was holding gushed out of her as Grant rose and let Tabitha pull him toward the center seat at the counter. Then the girls scrambled onto the seat on either side of him, grinning at their victory. God really was showing off today.

Meg pulled the dome off the cake with a flourish and lit the single candle.

"Just one?" Grant asked.

"I thought it best not to guess," Meg admitted.

"And I thought it best not to tell," Cay added.

But Sadie was having none of it. "How old are you?"

Grant pursed his lips for a moment, then to Meg's surprise made a big show of pretending to count it off on his fingers. "I'm thirty-two."

Tabitha scrunched up her face. "That's old."

"Is not!" Cay countered. "That's not even close to old."

"Neither are you," Meg felt compelled to add.

Tabitha tugged on Grant's elbow. "Quick, make your wish."

Meg expected a man like Grant to dismiss such a thing. Instead, his face took on the oddest expression. As if he were genuinely considering his wish. She found herself fascinated at the way he looked with his eyes closed, the closest thing she'd seen to hope ever on his face. She told herself it was for the girls' sake, but she couldn't quite convince herself of it. Time halted for the briefest of moments before his eyes opened again and he blew the candle out.

"What'd you wish for?" Tabitha asked.

"You're not supposed to tell, silly," Sadie warned from Grant's other side.

Grant shrugged. "Those are the rules."

Despite the rules, Meg found she very much wanted to know what Grant had wished for. Whatever it was, she hoped it gave him a little bit of happiness. He hadn't smiled—at least not yet—but she liked to think the girls' gesture would do the trick before this impromptu party was over.

"First slice goes to the man of honor," she

declared as she cut an extra-thick slice of cake and tilted it onto a plate to set in front of Grant.

He took the fork from her hand, their fingers touching for the briefest of moments as he did. There was no reason to react the way she did, noticing the contact, being so aware of the touch. Still, it felt…important. More intense than a casual touch handing off flatware should feel. The small zing served as an unwelcome reminder that she did feel an attraction toward him, irrational as it was.

She was lonely and stressed, she told herself. And he was handsome, and the girls, for some reason, adored him. None of that was anything she should act on. It wasn't the right time, and he certainly wasn't the right man.

So why had she gone to such lengths to throw an impromptu birthday party for the wrong man?

Because he needs it, came the reply from somewhere deep in her spirit. And that was what she did at the Sundial. She fed people's needs. And not just with food. Feeding others had become her path out of the grief, her way to stay out of the self-pity that lurked around her in the evenings after the day was done and the girls were sleeping. This was just another serving of… well, service. How God wired her to be in the world. And why the thought of missing any payment on the loan and endangering the house or

the diner struck her with bone-deep fear. The
Sundial was her lifeline.

"Wow," Grant exclaimed, pulling her out of
her thoughts and back to the moment. "Anyone
ever tell you that you make a really good cake?"

His praise warmed her. "Right after they tell
me how good my coffee is. Mike's a great cook,
but I know it's the cake and pie that brings 'em
back."

"We helped," Sadie chimed in, fishing for
praise of her own.

"Both of us," added Tabitha, never one to be
left out.

"I have no doubt you did," Grant said. Again,
Meg noticed how he spoke to them with respect. Like children, yes, but as if they were
just smaller-sized humans and not someone to
be dismissed or talked down to.

Grant hoisted his fork. "Well, I am going to
enjoy this delicious cake you made for me." He
took another big bite as if to prove his point.

"Then you gotta walk around," Tabitha in-
structed. She noticed the girls treated Grant the
way he treated them. Not as some big, impos-
ing figure, but just a larger-sized human who
needed a better outlook on the world. As if they
had things to offer him.

"You think I need exercise?" Grant asked. It
came delightfully close to a joke.

The girls giggled. "No, silly," Tabitha replied, "You gotta let everyone say happy birthday to you."

Grant did not look as if he found that a pleasing prospect. "Nah, I'm good."

"Nope," Tabitha insisted. "It's the rules."

"Whose rules?" Then Grant turned to look at Meg as if he didn't need the girls to tell him.

She simply smiled. "Had it been a regular cake, the rules don't apply. But seeing as it's a birthday cake..."

"Wait a minute. You were going to make a cake before someone let on it was my birthday?"

Meg was trying to figure out how to answer that when Sadie did it for her. "You needed cake."

Grant made a show of checking his ribs. The man was fit and muscular—he didn't need any beefing up, by baked goods or any other means. "Why do I need cake?"

This was not the time and place to get into the girls' diagnoses of Grant's broken smile. Meg quickly set two smaller slices in front of the girls. "Mr. Grant can't eat his cake if you keep asking him questions. Let him eat his slice. Then you can take him around to get his happy birthdays from people."

Remembering Grant's strong resistance to come into the diner, it struck Meg that his lone-wolf tendencies had cost him a great deal. She knew something about that isolation. She'd burrowed herself away after Andy died, and it had been the wrong impulse. Grant hadn't even realized what drove him back to High Mountain. He needed to reconnect, to find community again. Today, cake was how that happened. Hopefully, God would send other ways into his life.

One of those ways shouldn't be her, but as she watched Tabitha and Sadie escort Grant from table to table, reluctantly accepting birthday wishes, Meg knew her girls could play a part.

Chapter Ten

There were good kinds of tired and bad kinds of tired. Today left Meg the good kind of tired. The well-used, been-of-service kind of tired that was always best treated with a long sit on the front porch watching the stars come out. Meg thought, for just a moment, how nice it would be to have a loyal dog curled in companionship by her feet at a time like this. Maybe someday.

The girls had been excited all evening, hyped up by all that frosting and the chance to be in the spotlight with Mr. Grant. What a joy it had been to watch them drag—yes, *drag* was the word—Grant from table to table, insisting he listen to every person in the diner wish him a happy birthday.

He'd been serenaded by aunts, cousins, people who'd known him as a child or in school, and perfect strangers. For the kind of recluse she guessed Grant to be, it was an ordeal. Still, Meg was sure she spied a small smile or two creep across the man's face by the end of the day. Es-

pecially when each girl gave him a celebratory
kiss on the cheek. His cheeks flushed just a bit,
and he made a show of grumpily enduring the
pecks, but there was no hiding how the party
had touched him.

It was about way more than cake. Those things
always were.

Back when Meg first opened the diner, she'd
arranged for something called Heart Meals with
Pastor Jim. It was crucial to her that the diner
show generosity, even if it was a stretch. Maybe
especially when it was a stretch…like now. She
couldn't donate meals outright, but she'd asked
the church mission fund to cover just the food
costs for a handful of meals a month. When
someone came into the diner clearly in need—
financially or emotionally—Meg would present
that person with one of the Heart Meal vouchers.
It meant they could eat without paying. Sometimes the pastor sent people to her; other times
God did the sending, showing her which of her
customers needed extra care. Heart Meals reminded Meg of her purpose at the Sundial, of
how God always provided.

Today hadn't involved any Heart Meals, but it
had met the same deep unspoken need for Grant.
She was sure of it. So while she was tired as she
sat in the rattan porch rocking chair after the

girls were bathed and asleep, she wasn't weary. That was a gift in itself.

Meg looked up to see a figure walking across the field between her house and the farm. It took only a few seconds to recognize the towering silhouette and the powerful walk: Grant.

The prospect of him on her porch in the starlight hummed within her in unwelcome ways. He'd never sought her out, never visited her anywhere but the diner, and always on the pretense of coffee or food. None of those things could apply to tonight's visit.

With an irrational vanity, she wondered what she looked like—hair frizzed from getting the girls bathed, shirt stained from dinner and an errant glass of grape juice, the day's makeup long gone. She ought to turn on the porch light and dispel the intimacy of darkness, but that would only let him see her disheveled appearance more clearly. It was tough to decide if the shadows were friend or foe.

She opted to keep the light off, choosing to hide in the just-enough moonlight and the wedges of yellow glow from the house windows behind her.

Grant crossed the final yards to stand at the foot of her porch stairs. Manners dictated she invite him up to sit on the other chair, to offer him something to drink or some such hospitality. Meg found herself too afraid to do it. Having him seek her out and stand on the edge of her porch proved challenge enough. *Lone wolf* was an apt description of the man; moonlight definitely suited him.

He'd clearly come to say something, so she waited for him to speak.

"I came to say thank you." Although he spoke softly, the words carried great weight. "For the cake…and…everything."

"I was pleased to do it," she replied. That was true. She did enjoy the party, a little more than she was ready to admit. "But the girls were right—it was their idea. Before we learned it was your birthday."

Grant shook his head. "Yeah, Mom's been on about that. The whole 'God showing off' thing."

His tone hinted at a large dose of skepticism. "You don't think God does things like that?"

"Not for me." The quick reply let his deep conflict emerge. Grant Emerson was a man who put holes in walls but was tender to puppies and little girls.

She felt brave enough to press him. "So you think the girls getting the notion you needed cake right at the time of your birthday is just coincidence?"

Grant ran a hand through his hair. "I don't know what I think about today."

She didn't, either. All sorts of thoughts had been tumbling in her mind. She was grateful the diner had enjoyed a brisk business, but today had been about much more than that.

He leaned against her porch column, shoulders easing out of their constant tension. "You stopped the girls from telling me why I needed cake. I got the sense they knew the answer. Mind telling me what it is?"

So he *had* noticed. Did she really want to go there with him? Did she have a choice? It was clear he'd walked across the field for more than a thank-you. *I hope You know what You're doing here, God*, she prayed as she considered how to answer.

Grant caught her hesitation. "Well? If it's something awful, trust me, I've heard worse."

Somehow she knew that was true. Not just because of his job—which surely must show him the worst of what humanity can do—but something deeper. It couldn't be family. Cay's home was a house of love. Grant and Ivy must have had lovely childhoods growing up on that farm.

She offered an apologetic smile. "I'm not so sure you'll like the answer."

To her surprise, he lowered himself down to sit on the top step. Settling in to listen to whatever it was she was about to tell him. When the girls blurted outrageously true things, as they too often did, their sweet innocence often let them get away with it. Meg doubted that worked with grown adults.

She pulled in a deep breath and started at the beginning. "We were talking Thursday night about why Daisy likes you so much."

Grant almost laughed and shook his head. "Yeah, that stumps me, too. I'm not exactly the warm, fuzzy type."

At least he acknowledged his prickly nature. "I think animals pick up on things. They know who needs—" She almost said *to be loved*, but decided that was a bit much for a man like Grant "—attention. Even when the rest of us might not see it."

He scrunched his face up in a way that resembled Sadie. "Not seeing the cake connection here."

"I'm getting to that." Meg got up off the chair and walked to the porch railing, being careful to stand a safe distance from Grant. Not because she was afraid of him, but she was wary of the feelings he seemed to stir up. "Tabitha and Sadie decided that Daisy likes you because, according to my daughters, your smile is broken. It doesn't work right like Daisy's hind legs don't work right. And that's why Daisy likes you. You both have broken parts."

She watched Grant's reaction carefully. He

didn't respond right away, but he did let his head fall back against the column behind him.

"I've had a lot of things said about me, but that is the first time I've ever been accused of having a broken smile." Almost as if to prove his point, his reply had the tone of a joke, but he did not show even a hint of a grin.

"They're not wrong. I mean, I'm not sure that's why Daisy takes to you, but you've been here three weeks and been exposed to all kinds of adorable cuteness between the girls and the puppies—you've even had a surprise birthday party thrown for you—and you have not smiled."

He actually looked surprised at that. "Not once?"

"Not even once. A sort of, kind of, hint of a grin at the diner this afternoon, but a full-out smile? Never." She leaned against the railing and crossed her arms over her chest. "You probably have a really nice one, but who would ever know?" Meg suddenly regretted saying that last bit. She had thought a man as handsome as Grant Emerson probably had a dashing smile, but that didn't mean she needed to tell him so.

He stared at her, puzzled. "So cake is the way to repair a broken smile?"

"If you're five and six years old, yes. Come to think of it, it works if you're thirty-two years old, too."

Grant looked up at the darkened upstairs windows. "Are the girls disappointed that their cake repair didn't work?"

She liked that he wasn't insulted—more concerned that the girls had been disappointed. "More puzzled than upset." Such odd glimpses of compassion in a man so otherwise dark and distant. She sensed he was capable of caring—of showing great care—but it had somehow been tamped down so far inside him that he didn't know how to let it out.

"Well, I suppose I've got to fix that." Grant sat up straight, pulled in a deep breath and proceeded to apply the most forced, ridiculous so-wide-it-was-almost scary smile.

Meg burst out laughing. "I don't know what that was, but it was *not* a smile."

"Sure it was." Again, the tone of a joke, but his face fell back into its constantly serious expression.

"No, sir, it was not." She pointed at him. "That's the kind of smile that makes people afraid of clowns. Which the girls considered, by the way. Painting a smile onto your face. Be glad I talked them out of it."

"I'll thank you for that. Cake's a far better choice. And it was really good cake."

She thought it needed saying. "When you do smile for the girls, let it be the real thing. A genuine smile. Because you're happy about something."

He nodded. "Deal. Might take a while."

"Seems fair." His agreement gave her the courage to break a birthday rule. "Since I answered your question, will you answer one of mine?"

He gave her own words back to her. "Seems fair."

"You chose your birthday candle wish pretty carefully. What was it?"

He gave her a dubious look. "I thought you weren't supposed to tell."

"When you're five and six years old, yes. But I think we're safe."

That sent a shadow across his features. "Interesting choice of words, that."

"How so?"

He paused so long before answering Meg thought he wouldn't offer up his wish. He ran a hand across his chin, and she could tell he was choosing his words carefully. Whatever he was going to say, it was important. Might it have to do with the reason behind Grant's broken smile?

"I seem to leave a lot of…damage…behind. My life has a lot of nasty baggage. Part of it's the job, but part of it…well, is me."

Again, it was hard to imagine Cay Emerson's son saying such things about his life. Meg stayed

silent, giving him space to say whatever would
come next.

"And now I'm here. And everyone is so nice.
Mom and the family…" He looked up at her, and
she read the unspoken *And you* in his gaze. It
sent a delicate jolt through her insides. Part cau-
tion, part something else.

"So I was wishing that all that damage
wouldn't follow me here."

Grant wanted to pull the words back. To turn
around and run back across the field as fast as he
could. Anything to fight against the totally out-
of-control feeling his admission to Meg pulled
up in his chest.

He hadn't said what he was really thinking. *I
wreck things and I don't want to wreck you. Or
the girls. Why do you think I'm in such a hurry
to leave?* There was no way he could say that.
Ever. Not to her or to Mom or to any of the people here.

What Mullins had told him at the diner confirmed he'd been right. The dirty cops went
high up in the department. He'd been targeted.
Knowing what he knew, he presented a threat.
Threatened people who had a lot at stake went
to extremes. They didn't know he was here, but
how long would that last? Staying here might
seem safe for him, but it put High Mountain at

risk. Even going back to Billings and pressing his case could put High Mountain at risk.

Stay or go? Press or back off? No one would understand the battle going on in him every single moment. The need to go back and wage war in Billings clashed with Luke's warning to sit tight in High Mountain until he had a better battle plan.

And people wondered why he never smiled?

He stood up, the look on her face almost pushing him off the porch. "I should go."

A ridiculous part of him wanted her to say, "No, stay." It was dark and peaceful on her porch, and he could tell himself the lie that he *could* stay. So much of him was starting to *want* to stay.

But of course, she didn't ask him to stay. How could she after he'd just admitted his talent for damage? He was very good at protecting, but justice always came with costs. To him. To others.

Grant didn't believe in curses, but he did believe some lives were destined to be dark and heavy. A man didn't have the right to invite someone else into that kind of life. Instead, you build high, sturdy walls so that people are protected from it. And you never peek out, because if you do, you start to want what's on the other side. What you can't have.

Chocolate cake and puppies and little girls who think they can fix your broken smile. Extraordinary women like Meg.

He started to back off the porch, half turned toward the farm, but not all the way because he couldn't seem to pull his eyes from the look on Meg's face. It was one thing to know you were a liability. It was another to watch someone recognize it. To watch her know he didn't—couldn't ever—belong in her life.

"Grant?"

Why did she have to say his name like that? With all that struggle and determination and kindness?

"Thank you."

She was thanking him? He'd come here to thank *her*. "For what?"

"For telling me what you wished."

How could she be grateful when every bone in his body regretted the admission?

"I'm glad I know."

There it was. The understanding of what followed him around in this world. It was done; the wall had been raised higher, and there'd be no more peeking over at the sunny side.

"I'm glad you know, too," he replied. And he was.

Only he wasn't.

Chapter Eleven

Grant sat in front of the window in his old bedroom Monday afternoon, compiling evidence. He filled a notebook with everything he knew, had seen or suspected about what was going on back in Billings. Dates, pieces of conversation, inconsistencies, missing files, lapses in procedure that looked innocent alone until you started lining them up. He'd always been good with names and dates, but it wasn't smart to depend on memory for something like this. If he went back and took what he knew to an Internal Affairs hearing—and he was pretty sure now he'd have to go that high, if not higher—he'd need all the concrete evidence he could muster. People like this, officers who had risen far enough up in the ranks to abuse this kind of power, knew how to cover their tracks. After all, who was more skilled at breaking the law than someone who defended it?

Only he wasn't making much progress. Not because he didn't have a long list of things to write down, but because he kept staring out the window at Tabitha, Sadie and Meg. They'd come over to play with the puppies like they did nearly every day after school.

He had the window open so that he could hear all the happy sounds. Revel in the giggles and barks, the squeals and yelps, the particular sound of Daisy's wheels bumping over the grass. He ought to move away from the window and get some solid work done, but he couldn't bring himself to do it.

He heard the sound of his mother's footsteps behind him, and turned to see her leaning against the doorway he'd left open.

"What are you doing all the way up here?" she asked in an all-too-parental voice.

He quickly snapped the notebook shut. "Work." It was, sort of. Just unofficial. Something that was just as likely to tank his career with the force as advance it—depending on who believed him.

"So you're not on vacation."

He limited his reply to a soft grunt.

Mom sat down on the bed. Grant didn't care for how it echoed back to when she'd come into his room as a young boy to ferret out what was bothering him. Despite her introverted, scientific nature, his sister, Ivy, was an open book. If she trusted you, it was hard to get her to stop talking and analyzing everything. On the other hand, Mom used to say it took a jackhammer to get anything out of him. She wasn't wrong.

"The girls are asking me why you aren't coming out to play." She smirked. "Their words, not mine. Want to tell me how I should answer their question?"

"That I'm too old to come out and play?" He knew the joke wouldn't placate her, but it was worth a try.

Mom fussed with the sleeve of her shirt. "Then let's try my words. Why are you hiding up here when it's clear as day you want to be down there?"

"I don't want to be down there."

Mom's response was a powerful *Don't you lie to me* face. Jenkins, the best interrogator in the department, had nothing on that face.

He chose a useful truth. "I shouldn't be spending so much time with them."

"Why? The girls adore you." She pointed to the window. "Just listen to that. It's my favorite sound. It's a blessing that the farm isn't so quiet anymore. Don't you agree?"

A fresh peal of laughter floated in through the window. A painful counterpart to the hard, cold feeling in his chest.

"Are you ever going to tell me the real reason you are out here?" Mom squared off at him—no small feat, since he was standing and she was still sitting on the bed. "I'm glad to have you under my roof, but if whatever is going on is as serious as you're trying not to tell me, then I think I have a right to know."

She was probably going to have to know at some point. He just had to figure out the least possible amount of facts to reveal. He settled on stalling. "Do I have to tell you now?"

"Well, I'd rather you did."

That fell happily short of a demand. "I need to think on it."

"Sweetheart, you've done nothing *but* think on it since you got here. And maybe that's half your problem. Everything building up inside. Feeling like you can't trust anyone, even your own mother. It'd break anybody's smile."

When he glared at her, she waved a hand. "Yes, I know about that broken-smile business. Those girls don't keep any secrets. Maybe that's why they're so much happier than you are."

They're happier than me because they're not assessing whether or not departmental corruption is fixing to harm me or my career, he argued in his mind. "I'm fine, Mom."

Now she stood up. "You are the furthest thing from fine. I know it, you know it, they know it. So answer me this, young man—" she pointed at him "—and you'd best tell me the truth when you do."

How did she do that? Make a six-foot-five, two-hundred-twenty-four-pound man feel small?

"What?" His voice came out sharper than it ought to. Some huge, dangerous question was about to be thrust at him, and he couldn't think of a single way to stop it.

"Did the cake help?"

What? They were talking about how well he was concealing the largest threat to his career to date, and Mom asks about *cake*? "The cake?"

"Yes," Mom said as if it were a perfectly normal question. "Did it help?"

He didn't have to think about it. Still, it bothered him—immensely—to admit the answer. "Yes," he said quietly, reluctantly.

Mom looked pleased. "See? That wasn't so hard."

What on earth was happening to him here?

"Did whatever you were doing just now help?"

She had a point. Documenting the extent of his knowledge and suspicions only raised his blood pressure. It helped in that it was necessary, but it absolutely made him feel worse. "Not especially."

"Well, then, any intelligent son of mine would figure out that the place to be isn't up here—it's down there."

But she's down there. He was starting to feel drawn to Meg. Like some giant emotional rubber band, the harder he pushed away, the stronger the pull toward her became.

He had no idea what to do about it.

After the lunch rush on Tuesday, Meg watched Grant's truck pull up in front of the diner with a very large box in the back.

She was surprised to see him. Ever since that admission on the porch Saturday night, it was as if he was trying to keep his distance from her and the girls. Well, more distance than the usual mile-high emotional walls the man walked around carrying. Even the girls noticed how some of the little ease he'd had had left him.

She'd become more convinced that his birthday-candle wish had failed to come true. Whatever he'd wished wouldn't follow him here had already arrived. Still, she was glad to see him. She'd missed him—even though she'd never admit it to anyone, barely even herself.

"Got a delivery for you," he said as he struggled to get the enormous rectangular box through the diner door. "From Mom. For the Hot Dogs for Dogs thing."

Meg put down the napkin container she was filling and walked over to where Grant set it down. "She didn't tell me to expect anything. It's huge."

"And heavy. She didn't tell me what it was, either, only that I had to go pick it up at the hardware store and bring it here."

Meg peered at the box. It looked large enough to hold one of those fancy flat-screen televisions. Or a big piece of art. She couldn't image Cay buying either of those, much less needing it delivered here. "Wally could have brought it over, whatever it is. You didn't need to come into town for this."

"Mom insisted I had to bring it, and I had to be here when you open it."

It didn't take police investigative skills to see Cay was likely inventing reasons to get her and Grant together. Every time Meg saw Cay, some small hint would find its way into the conversation. Something along the lines of Grant needing the right woman in his life or how sweet it was how the girls had taken such a shine to him.

Having already fended off a similar speech from Barb, Meg had no doubt Peggy would join the matchmaking campaign soon enough. If the girls caught wind of the sisters' ideas, it'd be five against two. Five and a half, actually, because part of Meg was ignoring her better judgment and thinking of Grant all too much.

"Shouldn't your mom be here?"

"I said the same thing. She insisted someone had to stay home with the puppies."

Although Meg knew the answer, she asked, "Why couldn't it be you?"

"For one thing, it's too big. Mom could never hoist this thing, whatever it is. For another, she said I needed to watch you see it for the first time. She's seen it, I guess."

Meg walked around the box, now leaning up against a table. "So what is it?"

"Only one way to find out." He pulled out a pocket knife, and with precise strokes he cut the side of the box open. He tugged out a bit of brown paper wrapping. Looking inside the box, he grumbled something indistinguishable and reached in. He slowly pulled a large rectangle, straight at the bottom and arched at the top, all wrapped in more brown paper.

"Oh no." Grant said. "She didn't."

"She didn't what?" What could Cay have ordered to be delivered to the Sundial for the Hot Dogs for Dogs fundraiser? It was too hefty to be posters or fliers—the thing was enormous.

With one hand, Grant caught one end of the wrapping and pulled it off the object. A large red 3 peered out from the arched top, followed by the words *Sisters* underneath.

Realizing what it was, Meg couldn't decide

if she should applaud or clap her hands over her open mouth.

An enormous sign that said *3 Sisters Rescue Farm* came out from the wrapping. Cay, Barb and Peggy had announced their arrival in a very big, very permanent way.

"I guess they mean business," she offered with a chuckle at Grant's scowl. "It's so..."

Grant stood back, one hand on his hip, one hand running across his jaw in stunned disbelief. "Big," he finished for her.

"Sturdy," she added, not knowing what else to say. "And it's...well, it's charming?" The thing did have a rustic, friendly flair. But the whopping size definitely sent the message, "We're here. For good."

Grant just stared. Meg wasn't sure if she should be impressed at Cay's scheme to have Grant deliver it here or feel as if she was losing control of the situation.

"Wally at the store told me she ordered this five weeks ago."

Five weeks? "That's before the puppies arrived."

"Yep."

"You never had a chance of talking her out of this."

"Nope."

Meg was so busy being surprised at the big

wooden sign she nearly forgot an important question. "But why is it *here*? Shouldn't you be taking it home to the farm?"

At that moment, Peggy came through the diner door, face breaking into a wide smile at the sight of the sign. "Isn't it wonderful?" she said, grabbing Grant's arm. "It's just like I thought it would be."

"But why is it here?" Meg repeated. The thing would take up a whole corner of the room, and she wasn't so hard up for cash that she was selling advertising space in the diner. Well, not yet.

"So everyone can see it at the fundraiser," Peggy answered. "You can stand it up out front. It's rather big, so we didn't see the need to move it to the farm and back again."

Grant glared at his aunt. "A picture would have worked, Aunt Peggy."

Peggy ran her hand with affection over the large red number three. "Oh, not this well. No picture would have done this justice." Then, in a very poor imitation of someone who just happened to remember something, Peggy said, "Oh, that's right. I'm supposed to buy you lunch, Grant. As a thank-you for making the delivery."

"I don't need to have lunch with you, Aunt Peggy."

"Oh, you're not having lunch with me. I've got a church-committee meeting in twenty minutes. I just couldn't resist coming over and seeing our beautiful sign. And picking up your tab." She handed Meg an envelope. "Meg, honey, feed this strapping young man whatever he wants for lunch today." She put a hand on Meg's arm and leaned in. "My version of one of your charity lunches. I know you'll take the best care of him."

Grant raised an eyebrow at the phrase "charity lunches." It reminded Meg again that he was the only person outside her accountant who knew just how tight funds had become. He'd already voiced his concerns about the irrationality of Hot Dogs for Dogs. This was never about money, and she wasn't in the mood to hear Grant wet-blanket the idea again.

Peggy didn't give him the chance. She offered the sign one more loving caress, stood on tiptoe to kiss Grant on the cheek and swept out the door.

Grant stared after her. "My family's gone off the rails."

Meg could only laugh. "They certainly are characters. Bold women. I hope my girls have their gumption when they grow up." In truth, she craved the sisters' bold optimism as she faced all her current challenges.

"Gumption?" Grant raised an eyebrow at the down-home term.

"What would you call it?"

He leaned down to peer at the sign more closely. "Oh, I don't know. A few choice words come to mind."

She laughed again. "Well, you get credit for not saying any of them out loud. It is your family, after all." It took Meg a moment to work out where in the diner the huge sign could fit. "I guess we can put it over there by the window. I was going to put out some fliers, but I surely won't have to with that thing in the corner."

Mike came out from the kitchen and gave a long, low whistle. "What is that?"

"That," Grant said as he finished pulling the last of the wrapping paper from the sign, "is a classic McNally sisters' scheme."

"It's enormous," Mike said.

"Really," Grant said, tilting his head to the side. "I hadn't noticed. Can you give me a hand?"

Together, the two men maneuvered the large sign through the maze of tables until it stood up against the wall by the diner's front window. Meg pictured the sun coming up over the mountains, kissing the top of the sign every morning. If they put it by the front drive, she would see it from her kitchen window. She liked that idea.

Sign duly installed, Grant began to gather up the packaging and beeped his key fob to unlock the truck.

"Where do you think you're going?"

"Home to give my mother a piece of my mind."

"Oh, no," she countered, pleased to have an excuse to keep him in the diner a bit longer. Had the three sisters schemed that as well? "I have to feed you lunch."

"No, you don't."

She waved the envelope at him. "I've been paid in advance. This isn't negotiable."

He halted, and she could see him choose to give in to Peggy's ploy. Something almost akin to a smile flashed across his face. "Well, I'm probably better off arguing with Mom on a full stomach, anyways." He sat down on a counter stool.

He always sat on the center stool. She liked the idea of him being a diner regular. She liked having him in her life—not too deeply in her life, but along the edge. And then there was how much the girls liked him.

Meg reached down to a shelf below the counter and produced the great big coffee mug she'd never admit she kept special just for him. "What'll it be, big fella?"

Chapter Twelve

Mike handed Grant an apron and an enormous set of barbecue tongs. "Thanks for the help tonight, man." It was Wednesday night, and the Hot Dogs for Dogs fundraiser at the diner was about to kick into high gear.

Grant shrugged. "I'd rather be here than out there schmoozing donors, but I can't see why you need help. Don't you do this stuff every day?" In all the meals he'd had at the diner, Grant had come to admire the way Mike juggled orders. Perfect timing and a good cook to boot.

"That's work. I'm donating my hours tonight, so I'd rather not do this alone." He twirled the spatula in his hand with the flamboyance of a parade's grand marshal.

Mike, along with a whole host of other folks the three sisters had roped into service, were donating their time as cooks, servers and hosts. There was even someone making balloon-animal dogs. Anyone eating outside was invited to have their dog join them, and Meg had set out bowls of water and treats for canine customers. It all had the air of a carnival, complete with strings of lights.

Sadie walked up to Grant with a frown. "It'd be so much better if the puppies were here."

"Remember what Dr. Vicky said," he reminded the pouting girl. "They can't meet a whole bunch of other dogs until they've had all their shots. Besides," he added, looking around at the noise and activity, "I think it might be a bit much for them."

"But Hot Dogs for Dogs is *for* them," Sadie pleaded.

Grant pointed over to the big *3 Sisters Rescue Farm* sign up against the wall. "It's for the whole farm. For them and whoever comes after that." He surprised himself by admitting, out loud, his ability to see the farm's future. Was it still a huge uphill battle? Yes, but he was slowly gaining confidence in his mother's ability to rally both her sisters and the town. Wasn't tonight evidence of that? But what about Meg? How much was this costing her in profits while her diner was barely scraping by?

Sadie pondered his earlier remark. "Who do you think comes next on the farm?"

Grant had to laugh. "I'm not sure I want to think about that." He caught a glimpse of Mom gliding through the crowd. He hadn't truly realized how much her sparkly spirit had faded until he'd watched its return lately.

"I have," Sadie countered. "I think it should be goats. The little kind that jump around."

And eat everything in sight, Grant added in his mind. "Grandma Cay says whoever is next is whoever God sends." Again, he marveled at how repeating his mother's farm theology came with astonishing ease.

Sadie clapped her hands together in the classic child prayer pose. "Okay, I'm gonna pray God sends goats."

I'm gonna pray God takes His time. "How about we get the puppies grown up a bit more before we ask God to send anyone else?" He tugged gently on one of Sadie's blond braids. Talking with the girls had become one of his favorite things. He'd stopped trying to stay away when they came to the farm, giving in to the— yes, he was going to name it what it was—*fun* he had with them.

As Sadie skipped off, Grant's eyes found Meg in one corner of the diner, taking orders. Since the diner wasn't normally open for dinner, this was the first time he'd seen her in the Sundial after dark. The small yellow lights that had been strung up in the diner and outside on the sidewalk not only added to the festival atmosphere, it lit up the curls of her hair. She was having as much fun as Mom tonight, if not more. The woman fairly glowed.

The way Meg looked on the porch the other night—all soft and tender and cautious in the moonlight—had stuck with him. Her glow tonight called to him in a way he hadn't ever felt, and didn't trust. She was far from perfect—she was more frightened than her cheeky personality would ever tell—nor did she boast the bold, who-cares-what-anyone-else-thinks air of Aunt Barb.

But she was brave. He knew tonight represented a financial risk. He was pretty sure her situation was even more dire than she'd admitted to him. She needed every bit of profit she could eke out, and tonight she was giving those profits away. That was a kind of bravery and faith he could never hope to have.

Still, he very much liked being near it. And the need to protect it, to discover some way to make her money problems disappear, was becoming a challenge. Gazing at her from across the room like this, he knew that he had no answers for her. That didn't stop him from wanting to be an answer for her, yearning to protect her and the girls. He was losing the battle to tamp down his feelings for her, and he had no idea what to do about it.

She noticed him watching at just that moment,

a spark in her eye as if she'd heard his thought. She smiled, and he felt it hum through his chest. Unnerved, he busied himself with loading another batch of hot dogs onto the grill.

When he looked up not even a minute later, she was standing beside him, the softest of smiles lighting up her face. That was the thing about her—she had every reason to be hard and bitter, but she was so soft. Her voice, her smile, the tender way she spoke to the girls. Even when she was teasing him, she somehow softened the edge of it. Did she have any idea what that did to a man with a hard-edged life like his?

"The turnout's better than I'd hoped," she declared, looking around the crowded room. "Mike thought we'd bought too many hot dogs, but I don't think so. I hope we run out."

With an apologetic nod to Mike, Grant abandoned his post at the grill and pulled her aside. It was half to be nearer to her and half to say what he thought needed to be said. "Meg," he said the minute they were out of earshot of the others, "are you sure you should be doing this? Giving all this food away?"

She sighed. "Of course not. I can't afford this. On paper, anyway."

So she would admit it. The urge to make her see reason practically made him want to grab her shoulders. "Then why are you doing it? You said yourself that you can't take this kind of risk. Things are too tight for you and the girls." His inability to help her cut too sharp an edge into his tone.

She looked at him with a combination of surprise and hurt. "Of course I know things are too tight. I don't want to think about what might happen if I miss another payment on the house. But I told you before—I've been scraping by for so long I've forgotten what abundance feels like. I don't ever want to teach that kind of poverty to my girls. So while you may not be able to understand it, I can't afford *not* to do this."

He had no right to tell her what to do with her life. Still, it gnawed at him. "*Are* you losing money tonight?" He tried not to make the question a challenge.

Her eyes told him he didn't quite succeed. "I could have if no one showed up."

With his mother and aunts dragging everyone in town to the event, Grant didn't see that happening. "But you risked it anyway."

Something changed in her face. "For years, I drowned in risks. Andy's work, Andy's schemes, the next big investment bound to make us rich. I don't do risk anymore. Tonight was different."

"I don't see how."

Meg held his gaze. "You've never had God

drop a wild idea in your head and just bug you until you did it?"

"Mom talks that way about the farm, but me? No." He started to elaborate, to explain, but realized he couldn't. He didn't know why those sort of purposeful experiences passed him by.

"Well, maybe your turn is coming soon." She nudged his elbow, and the small touch evaporated all the tension between them. How did she do that? Why did he like it so much when she did? "Stop worrying about me. Mike needs help." She started to walk away, then turned back with a wink before adding, "And save one of those hot dogs for me."

"Good night, and thanks for coming!" Three hours later, Meg waved the last Hot Dogs for Dogs customer out the door. She turned to the trio of McNally sisters, Mike and Grant, who were cleaning up the tables behind her. One of the high school kids had taken Tabitha and Sadie back to the house so they could get to bed at a decent hour. "We did it, didn't we?"

Cay stopped what she was doing and rushed up to pull Meg into a tight squeeze. "We did, indeed." She turned to Peggy, who had been tallying up the receipts and the contents of the dog-shaped cookie jar that sat on the counter for extra donations. "How much good did we do, Peggy?"

Peggy had insisted Meg give her a full accounting of the diner's expenses. They had talked her into a plan to split the proceeds so that the Sundial took some profit from the evening, but Meg had already decided to ignore it. She was going to give her half over to the farm. Tonight felt too good to do anything less than that.

Peggy squinted into her reading glasses and punched a few more numbers on a calculator. "Very good," she replied.

"Mind putting a number on that 'very good,' sis?" Barb called as she tied a garbage bag closed.

"Backing out the food costs, two thousand three hundred twelve dollars and twenty-seven cents," Peggy proclaimed.

Barb gave a whoop. "That's almost twelve hundred a piece for the farm and the diner."

"Eleven hundred fifty-six and thirteen cents. Well, one of us gets fourteen cents."

"No. You get it all. I already decided," Meg declared. For the first time in forever, a risk felt exciting instead of terrifying. She had two weeks until the next loan payment. Surely God would provide, and it felt so very healing to be generous. If nothing broke and business stepped up just a little bit more, she could squeak by.

Grant's expression darkened instantly. "Mom, don't let her do that."

Cay chose now of all times to listen to her son. "I agree. Half the proceeds go to you, just like we agreed, Meg." She pointed to the sign on the wall that reminded customers half of all tonight's proceeds went to Three Sisters Rescue Farm. "Grant could arrest us for false advertising if we go back on our claim."

Grant glowered at his mother. "Technically, no, but do what Mom says anyway."

Cay walked over to Meg. "You've been more than generous, hon. Half is enough."

Enough. How often did her weary heart cry, *It's not enough*? Cay was telling her it was enough. She'd felt her joy returning tonight. And hadn't she just declared her trust that God would provide? What if that's exactly what He was doing? Wouldn't Grant be shocked to find she'd heard God's protection in his sharp warnings?

Suddenly it became easy to stick to the original agreement. The need to make some big, grand gesture dissolved. She'd wanted tonight to help her feel more hopeful, less pressed, and it had. "Okay then. Fifty-fifty it is." She watched relief fill Grant's features. He really had worried about her. That changed the way her spirit felt, too. "Honestly, tonight was the most fun I've had in months."

"Well, we certainly need to fix that," Barb

said as a conspiratorial look passed between the sisters. "Time for us three to call it a night."

"Once I check on the pups, I'm going straight to bed," Cay announced, rolling her shoulders and then yawning. "Mike, will you help me get these things into my car?"

"Mom, I'll help you," Grant cut in.

She waved him away. "No, no, you stay here and help Meg. I'm so glad you came in your truck so we can get that great big sign to its new home. You just head on back when you're good and ready. No one'll be waiting up for you." The unspoken *no hurry, you two* in her tone made Meg's cheeks heat up. The sisters were at it again.

Cay made a big deal of shooing Mike and her two sisters out the door. The waggle of eyebrows she sent Meg's way just as she pulled the door closed behind her was too much. While Meg was grateful for the quiet after a hectic day, it made being alone in the diner with Grant feel…close. She suddenly had a lot of things to say to him and no idea how to say them.

Grant stared after the closed door and pushed out a breath. "We need to do something about those three."

Meg certainly agreed, but what? How did you fend off matchmakers you weren't even ready to admit existed? "Ignore them and hope they go away?"

Grant eased himself onto one of the diner chairs. "Nah. They'll just take it up a notch." He glanced up at Meg. "I have talked to her, you know."

Meg laughed. "So have I. Well, I talked to your aunt Peggy. I don't think it did a lick of good." She reached under the counter for Grant's special mug. "There's some coffee left."

He rolled his shoulders. He'd worked hard tonight, and she appreciated it. "Yes, please."

The least she could do was indulge him. "And I just might have a slice of chocolate cake in back."

He actually grinned. She took a surprised satisfaction in how easily it came to his face. "Only if you've got two slices. No fun eating cake alone."

Meg was glad he didn't tell her to bring two forks. Sharing a slice, for some reason, felt too intimate. Something a couple would have done. "Who can resist a man who tells you you've got to eat cake?"

She regretted the tease instantly. After all, she'd bristled mere hours ago at him telling her not to overdo her generosity. And he'd been right. She didn't know how—or if—to thank him for that, either.

Still, she welcomed the banter between them. It felt close and caring. He'd shown her, in his own gruff way, that he cared about her. She missed having someone else looking out for her welfare. She missed having someone else, period. But she knew that someone else *shouldn't* be Grant Emerson.

Meg hid her regret by ducking into the back refrigerators to fetch out two slices of cake and a pair of forks. She set them on the counter and filled the large mug and a regular-size one with the last of the coffee, adding cream and sugar to hers as Grant rose and moved the cake to two seats in one of the side booths.

Half the diner lights were off, but the strings of lights hadn't yet been unplugged. Bright and cheery by day, the shadows and tiny golden bulbs made the diner seem…romantic. As if they were having dessert at a cozy restaurant. As if they were on a date.

Which they were not. Funny how she kept having to remind herself that.

"Grant…" she began, at the exact time he said, "Meg…"

He so rarely said her name. It shook something loose under her skin, making her feel off-balance even though she was sitting down.

They both flustered, which told Meg he felt whatever it was she was trying not to feel. "You first," Grant said unsteadily.

"I was going to say thank you. For being concerned about the diner." That felt safer than thanking him for his care about her. "I appreciate it."

Grant sank a fork into the cake. "You never needed to do any of this. Your girls saw good things tonight. They should see people taking care of you, too." When those words felt too close, he quickly added, "Customers. You know, regulars giving the diner their business."

Meg liked being able to count Grant among those regulars. "You've become a regular, you know." But for how long? She'd miss him when he returned to Billings.

"I like a good cup of coffee." He ate a piece of the cake, giving a little hum of appreciation. "And the cake's pretty good, too." He pointed to the oversized mug with his fork. "Who else gets the giant mugs?"

Busted. "Just you, actually. Never really seemed to fit anyone else before now." The admission felt close and personal. They held each other's gaze for a moment, then each had to look away and pretend to busy themselves with the cake.

"You're a good person, Meg." It had the same effect when he said her name the second time. "But tell me the truth about something?"

The question felt dangerous. Whatever he was going to ask, she felt as if she wouldn't be able to lie to him. "What?" The question came out more breathless than Meg would have liked.

"Are you and the girls going to get by? Money-wise?"

He was more like his mother than he realized. Just as persistent and more than a little pushy. It was best to tell him the truth. "I hope so."

She watched him ponder her vague answer. There was a warm admiration in his gaze she'd not seen before. There were flecks of amber in those steel gray eyes—or perhaps the lights were playing tricks on her. Perhaps lots of things were playing tricks on her.

"I wish there was a way I could… There's got to be some way I can…" Whatever he was going to say was cut off by the ring of his cell phone. Meg saw *Mom* flash on the screen when he pulled it out. She didn't know if she should be glad or annoyed Cay was checking up on them.

She couldn't make out the words, but Meg could hear Cay's tone of alarm.

"How?" Grant asked. "All of it? Could you get your car in down the drive?" A few more details from the other end of the line drew his face into a tight frown. "Okay. I'll be right there." He clicked off the call. "Can I get the coffee to go?"

She slid out of the booth at the same time he stood up. It brought them too close for a second, and they stepped apart instantly. "Of course," Meg said. "What's wrong?"

"Somebody must have run off the road earlier tonight. The gate to the farm's been knocked completely down."

Meg shook her head. "The way some people speed down these roads. She okay?"

"Mom's fine, but she can't get in the drive until I get there and pull the gate out of the way."

"Who does that kind of damage and drives away?" She had to pull two paper cups to hold the full amount of coffee in the mug. "Leave the sign here until tomorrow. You need to get over there, and I'm getting kind of used to it in the window."

"Thanks." Their hands touched again as she handed off the pair of coffees. "For everything."

She'd been in the diner alone at night dozens of times. But tonight, as she locked the door behind Grant, it felt lonely.

Chapter Thirteen

Grant's truck headlights put the farm front gate—or what was left of it—into view a few minutes later. The thing was flattened as if a tank had run it over.

"What happened?" he asked as he got out of the truck.

"I've no idea. People have gone off the road and dented the fence before, but never like this. I hope they're okay, whoever they are." Mom peered up and down the road as if she'd find someone injured in the ditches.

"I'm amazed they could drive away, actually." Grant began to fetch a coil of rope out of his truck. "You'd think they would at least leave a note."

"Probably too shocked or scared. Some young kid taking the corner too fast. Burt down the road had a whole corner of his fence knocked over last month. Never found out who did it."

Grant pulled out his phone and snapped a few pictures of the mangled chain-link fence.

"Are you going to put up a Wanted photo at the post office?" Mom half joked.

He couldn't believe Mom could make light of something like this. "It's for the insurance claim, Mom. You do have insurance, don't you?"

"*Of course* I do, son," she snapped, clearly not caring for his doubtful tone. "Aren't we glad this didn't happen with the brand-new sign? It's going up over there, and it might have been damaged."

Grant didn't find much to be glad about in the scene before him. This looked like an expensive repair. But the job right now was to move the broken gate so that Mom could get to her house. He began lashing the rope around the gate. "Give me a minute and I'll get this out of your way for now."

"I almost just left the car out here and walked down the drive. I didn't want to bother you while you were having a nice moment with Meg."

"We were not having *a nice moment*." He gave the words a vastly different tone than the emphasis Mom had. Not that it escaped him that the moment had, in fact, been nice. Really nice. "But that," Grant began as he tied off the knot, "is a conversation for later."

She waved him off. "Oh, we don't need to talk about it."

Grant glared at her as he checked the knot. "Oh, yes we do."

The gate, like so many other things on the farm, was old and creaky. He ended up having to pry it off its rusty hinges in order to clear the drive.

"This is too far gone," he declared as the tangle of metal and chain link finally came free from its hinges. "More likely a replace job than a repair job now."

"Well," Mom said as she nodded in agreement, "I expect we needed a new one, anyway."

"New ones cost more. And I doubt the insurance will cover all of it."

"We'll figure it out, son. Just get it out of the way for tonight."

Grant checked the ropes one more time. "Probably be a good thing to get you a motorized one. You won't have to get out and push it open and shut. When more animals come, good fencing and gates are gonna be important."

She stopped him halfway back to the truck, grabbing his elbow with a smile too wide for the situation. "What?" he asked.

"You said *when* more animals come. Not *if*."

Grant hadn't even realized his thinking had shifted that solidly. "Maybe I just figure this is gonna happen whether I like it or not."

She didn't say a word, just kept grinning as he gunned the truck and dragged the broken gate out of the way.

* * *

The next morning, while Mom was on the phone with the insurance company, Grant met with an officer from the local police department to file a report.

"I'm surprised the guy was able to drive away," the officer said as they stood out at the end of the drive, examining the tire tracks in the grass off the road. "He hit that gate hard. Kids drive reckless these days."

Grant scanned the road and the ditch. "He turned around." The tracks indicated a poorly executed three-point turn right in front of Mom's gate.

"Wouldn't you? Or whoever it was had a few too many and turned in the wrong gate. There's no sign or anything, and lots of these farms look the same in the dark."

"Mom's got a new sign made. I was actually supposed to bring it here last night. Before all this happened."

"Oh, right. The rescue animal thing. Sounds fun."

Fun wasn't the word Grant would use. "Only puppies for now, so we can get by until we put a new gate in."

The officer wrote a few more things in his report. "I'll make a note this one's a total loss.

Should help with the insurance folks. She's lucky she's got you to help her with this."

Grant had thought the same thing several times as he tried to get to sleep last night. Even the aunts, helpful as they were, wouldn't have been much help dealing with the gate last night and the paperwork today. He was grateful he was here. He was equally worried what would happen when he wasn't.

As he shook hands with the officer and pocketed the paperwork, Grant noticed three figures coming across the lawn. Meg and the girls. They were coming out to see both the puppies and what had happened with the gate.

Grant had expected he would see them today. What he didn't expect was how Sadie and Tabitha came running straight at him, attaching themselves to his legs with a wild, playful hug that nearly knocked him over. The unabashed affection caught him up short, and he just stood there, each leg practically wearing a giggling little girl.

"Aren't you supposed to be in school?" he asked with a mock-gruff voice.

"It's a sta-toot day," Tabitha explained.

"Institute day," Meg translated. "No school."

Grant tried to walk, or to make a half-hearted attempt to shake the girls off, but to no avail.

Sadie simply looked up at him, still giggling. "You're so big."

"You giggle a lot." He didn't know how else to respond. They'd always been playful, but they'd never plowed him over with hugs before. He didn't know how to hug them back, so he just patted each girl's shoulders. "Can I have my legs back now?"

That made them laugh more as they made a big show of releasing him. Meg smiled half in apology, half in amusement. She looked past him to the remains of the gate, now piled up against the fence in various pieces. "Looks bad. I'm glad nobody was hurt."

"Will the puppies get out and run away?" Tabitha asked, frowning at the pile of pipes and fencing.

"No. They stay in their pen, so they'll be fine." Not wanting to linger out here staring at the damage, he added, "Why don't you go over and see them while I take this paperwork back to Grandma Cay? We'll meet you out there in a bit."

The girls took off in the direction of the barn, but Meg held back for a moment. "Everything okay?"

"It'll be a big fix, but Mom seems to be taking it in stride. You know her—she found a dozen things to be grateful for."

"That's your mom, all right. High Mountain's champion optimist."

He found himself smirking. "Funny, I thought you held that title."

She shrugged. "I'm a happy second place. See you at the barn in a bit."

Something had shifted between her and Grant. It happened without their permission, and rather in spite of their best efforts to stop it. Meg had lain awake last night trying to sort through things, but her feelings were as jumbled and messed up as what was left of Cay's gate.

The girls, of course, didn't help matters. Something had shifted for them, too, as this morning's greeting displayed. What had made them run up to Grant and wrap themselves around the man like that? It took things to a different level. One Grant clearly wasn't comfortable with, yet she could still see how touched he was by the unabashed affection the girls gave him. It was how reluctantly charmed he looked, how it lit up his features in a way that just made a person want to light them up more.

"It's funny," Sadie said as they reached the barn entrance and pulled open the big doors. The puppies barked a greeting just as exuberant as the girls' had been. The whole litter—Daisy included—rushed over to push up against their pen as if they couldn't get to Tabitha and Sadie fast enough.

"What's funny, hon?" Meg asked as she carefully unlatched the pen gate and allowed the girls inside but took extra care to ensure no puppies escaped.

"We fixed Mr. Grant's smile, but Grandma Cay's gate went and broke," Sadie answered.

"That's how life works sometimes, isn't it?"

Sadie made a puzzled face, finding the thought a little too deep. She picked up one of the dozens of toys in the pen and began a fierce game of tug-of-war with the larger of the puppies. They were growing by leaps and bounds—except for Daisy. She didn't seem to grow as fast as the others, and Meg admitted to a bit of worry for the runt. Sometimes not every animal in a litter made it, but she didn't want her girls to have to learn a lesson like that right now.

The dog yanked at the toy, practically knocking Sadie over. "Bernard's getting really strong."

"They do grow," Meg offered, still a little distracted by the events of last night and this morning.

"We raised money for all of you last night" Sadie went on as she kept up the tugging battle with Bernard. "You shoulda been there. Everybody was there. Even Mr. Grant was there, all fixed."

Meg wondered what Sadie meant by that. "Fixed?"

Sadie looked as if that didn't need any explanation. "He's not grumpy anymore. We fixed it."

"Yes," Meg had to admit, "I suppose you did."

"Nah, mostly *you* fixed it." Tabitha seemed completely unaware of the weight of what she'd just said.

"Me?" Had the girls picked up on whatever it was growing between her and Grant? That didn't seem safe at all.

"You like him, don't you?" Sadie asked.

"He likes you," Tabitha added.

Meg willed her eyes not to widen. "Who told you that?"

"Grandma Cay. And Aunt Peggy. And Aunt Barb. Everybody thinks so."

Everybody? Or just three very persistent sisters? "That is not everybody's business," Meg answered. She hoped the girls did not pick up on the strength of her protest. Or the small corner of her heart that warmed at the news.

"I like him," Tabitha declared. "He's a big kind of nice. And not so grumpy now."

Meg had to admit, the description fit. "I think you two surprised him with that hug. But I think he liked it."

"Hugs are always nice," Sadie said, hugging

the nearest puppy. "You should give him one when he comes in."

Meg strove to keep the fluster out of her voice. "It's a bit different when grown-ups hug." It was more true that it was different when *certain* grown-ups hugged, but she wasn't going to get into that with the girls. It did, however, bring up how much she missed a true embrace. To lose yourself—even for a moment—in the strength of a man's arms. But *that* man's arms? For as strong as they were, it wasn't the right option. There, for a moment in the diner last night, with the glow surrounding them and all alone, if he had taken her into his arms, she might have let him.

And that would have been an enormous mistake. No, she had to be careful that her runaway emotions didn't pull her into foolish choices. Grant Emerson was everything she needed to be avoiding in life right now.

But what did you do when everything you should be avoiding lives right next door, adores your girls and looks like *that*?

As if summoned by her thoughts, Grant and Cay walked into the barn a minute later. The mother and son looked a bit bristly, as if they'd been arguing. They didn't say anything about it, but Cay kept throwing looks at Grant, who glowered in return. Were things tense on account of the gate accident? Surely the expense and the hassle would play right into Grant's arguments that the farm could be too much work for the sisters. It wasn't hard to envision a few hard conversations between the two of them.

"How are our puppies, girls?" Cay asked, a touch too brightly.

"They're growing fast," Sadie pronounced. "How big will they get?"

"You don't always know," Grant advised, walking to a side of the pen away from Cay. Which put him closer to Meg. Yes, there was certainly some friction between mother and son this morning. "Without knowing the mother and father, you can only guess."

"Dr. Vicky thinks they won't get more than thirty pounds," Cay explained. "Except for Daisy. She thinks Daisy will stay on the smaller side."

Grant squinted his eyes, calculating. "That's near two hundred and fifty pounds of dog, Mom. Sure you're up to it?"

Cay lifted her chin. "I raised you, didn't I?"

Meg hid her smile. *Cay: 1, Grant: 0.* She dreaded the day Tabitha and Sadie were old enough to press her like that. The girls were challenging in lots of other ways, but she was safe from the tension of teenage years and beyond...for now.

"I think they're hungry," Tabitha offered as

one of the puppies attempted a nibble on her shirt sleeve.

"I expect you're right. Kibble's out here, but I've got some extra chicken in the house. Want to help me bring it out, girls? There might be a doughnut in it for each of my assistants this morning."

The girls immediately scrambled to Grandma Cay's side, eager to help and earn their goodies. With a very pointed look that brought a frustrated near-growl from Grant, Cay and her helpers walked out of the barn, leaving Meg alone, again, with Grant.

He made another low sound and stood up to pace the small pen, picking up toys and rearranging straw.

"What was that all about?" Meg dared to ask.

"Mom and her meddling," he replied without looking up.

The McNally sisters were champion meddlers. The girls' conversation had proved that just moments ago. "All moms meddle," she offered for lack of a better response.

"Not on the level of that woman. I love her, don't get me wrong, but sometimes...." He left the sentence unfinished, tossing new straw from the bale behind the pen in among the puppies.

He looked like he needed to let off some

steam. "What's she poking her nose into your life about now?"

Grant totally surprised her by turning to look straight at her and declaring, "You."

Oh my. The sisters were turning things up a notch, weren't they? "Me?" she asked, even though she already knew the answer.

"Mom's got it into her head that you and I ought to…" He waved his hand in the air as if putting it into words was just too uncomfortable.

"Does she, now?" That answer seemed silly. Cay had been so blatant that it was ridiculous to pretend she hadn't caught on.

"Look…" Grant took a few steps toward her to stand shifting his weight as he spoke. "You… I… We both know it's a bad idea for a dozen reasons." He pushed the words out in a tortured rush.

Which meant he felt the same attraction and was fighting it just like her. In truth, the knowledge just made it worse. As if their mutual awareness of it grew stronger by him saying it out loud.

"Of course," she said too quickly. She did agree. It was just harder than she counted on. All the logic in the world didn't seem to add up to much in this case. She sat down on a nearby hay bale. "I mean, if you *really* lived here and did *anything* else for a living…"

Meg wanted to clamp her hand over her mouth. What had she just said? His blatant honesty had thrown her off-balance. By the impulsive naming of her objections, she'd basically admitted her attraction to him. She tamped down the childish urge to rush out of the barn and go hide in her house.

Grant pressed his lips together and shifted his weight again. "Well, I *don't* really live here, and I do what I do for a living."

Meg wrapped her arms around her knees, feeling foolish and vulnerable. "I get that."

He nodded. "Okay then, good. We're on the same page."

Meaning we both agree this...whatever this is...is a bad idea and we won't act on it? It didn't help much. Mostly because of those people back in the farmhouse, among others. What to do about them? "We still have a problem. Five of them, actually."

He raised an eyebrow, and Meg really didn't care for how the grumpiness charmed her. Eeyore, indeed. "Five?"

"I hate to tell you this, but all three sisters and both my daughters are in on it."

Alarm flashed across Grant's features. "What?"

"Tabitha just told me your mother and both your aunts told her you like me." The phrase *you like me* felt both childish and all-too-grown-up at the same time. Nothing about this made any sense whatsoever.

Grant let out a mortified breath and turned in a slow, confounded circle. "It's an ambush," he said. "We're outnumbered by old ladies and little girls in pigtails."

"Your mom is not old." Not the most important point at the moment, but still.

"She's old enough to know better," Grant fired back. He looked at his watch. "I've got to meet someone in an hour, but I think I'm leaving right now. When Mom comes back, tell her I'll deal with her later."

With that, Grant practically leaped over the pen's fencing and headed for the door at impressive speed.

Meg stared after the open doorway as she heard the sound of Grant's truck spitting gravel on its fast exit down the drive. *Whoever thought I'd see Officer Grump run?*

Chapter Fourteen

Grant had broken his own agreed silence and asked Luke for a meeting. He had to find a way to clear the path for him to get back to Billings, to find a way around the reason Luke was advising him to stay away. His return had to be soon, if not right away.

After making his escape from the barn, he arrived at the designated diner forty-five minutes early. He was glad to get out of High Mountain—too much was tangling around him back there. His feelings for Meg were edging out of his control. Mom's gate was busted. And now he found himself the target of five high-powered matchmakers who absolutely could not be allowed to succeed.

And to think, on his first day here, he'd thought a litter of puppies would be his biggest problem.

"For crying out loud, Emerson, you look worse than I expected."

Grant looked up from where he was frowning

into his mediocre coffee to see Luke standing over him. "Got a lot going on."

Luke slid into the opposite bench. "So I gathered. Tell me."

Grant crumpled the paper napkin at his place setting. "Police stuff first." He'd had an irritating craving for chocolate cake and ordered a slice of whatever the diner had. After a single bite, it sat in front of him uneaten, a lackluster substitute for another cake back in High Mountain.

"First? You mean there's more than just police stuff? Like what?"

Grant hadn't even realized he'd said "first." He didn't really know what had made him spit it out. "My mother and aunts and two little girls have decided I need a girlfriend." *Girlfriend*. There had to be a better word for the complex jumble of things he wanted Meg Kittering to be—or not be—in his life.

Luke's response was an immediate loud guffaw. "They're not wrong," his partner said, still laughing. "Man, that was the last thing I expected you to say."

"Oh, yes they are. Wrong. Dead wrong."

Luke, a ladies man who too often regaled Grant with his tales of romantic conquest, shook his head. "How many times have I told you that you needed a woman in your life to smooth over those rough edges of yours? So now half of High

Mountain's got someone in mind for you? I gotta meet her. And little girls? I'd pay good money to see that."

Grant glared at Luke. "You are not setting foot in High Mountain. Ever."

"Got under your skin that bad, huh?" Luke looked at the cake. "You gonna eat that?"

Luke's appetite for women was only exceeded by his appetite for food. The man would finish anybody's anything. It was department legend how many take-out meals, box lunches or casseroles Luke had polished off. Grant wordlessly slid the cake over to Luke's side of the table.

"Who is she?"

At first, Grant didn't want to answer. It was bad enough he'd admitted that everyone else in High Mountain thought he ought to like her. Still, he needed to work this out for himself, to talk through it with someone who wasn't Meg, the girls, his aunts or Mom. Right now Luke was his only available option. And his partner would probably bug him endlessly about it anyway.

"She owns the diner up there." He hadn't even realized until the words came out that he was squinting his eyes shut, as if the admission physically hurt. Like ripping off a bandage.

"Food always was the way to your heart," Luke teased.

"Actually, it was the coffee. She makes the most amazing coffee."

Luke smirked and hoisted his own mug. "Ah, now she's speaking your love language."

The mere mention of the *L* word made Grant's insides knot. "Do you have to put it that way?"

Luke held up his hands. "Touchy, are we? So, she's a mom? You mentioned little girls."

"Tabitha and Sadie." The memory of the girls hurtling themselves toward him and hugging his legs invaded Grant's thoughts. Heading back to Billings meant turning away from all that. Determined as he was, the cost of that return blindsided him. "Little kids." He heard their giggles echo in his mind. There wasn't another sound in the world like it.

"Hadn't pegged you for a little-kids guy. She must really be amazing."

"She's…she's…" He couldn't settle on a word. "…not a good idea."

"I'm not so sure I agree with that assessment," Luke said as he ate another bite of cake. "Tell me about her."

"Meg's husband was a test pilot killed in a plane crash. She admitted to me she's holding it together by her fingernails." Grant rubbed the back of his neck, half-relieved and half-mortified to be admitting this to anyone. "I'm the absolute last thing she needs."

Luke sat back in the booth. "Man, you are far gone. I've been waiting a long time to watch you fall for someone. Always thought you'd go down hard when you did."

Grant's back tightened. "I have not gone down hard."

Luke had an incredible talent for staring silently with a disbelieving face when he was sure a suspect was lying. He used that very face on Grant right now.

It worked as well as it had on the job. "Okay," he relented, "maybe I do think she's nice, but that doesn't change how things in no way line up for anything to happen. She needs a stable, no-risk guy who lives in High Mountain. Does that describe me?"

"Not in the slightest."

Grant sat back. "There you go."

Luke returned to leaning forward. "Doesn't matter. Or at least, it doesn't have to. The way you look when you talk about her? Or—and let's face it, this is more of a shocker—when you talk about those kids?" He shook his head again. "You've fallen for her."

It had become pointless to deny it. Maybe this was one of those things where it was better to face up to the problem and solve it. "Maybe," Grant nearly muttered.

"No *maybe* about it." Luke returned to polishing off the cake as if they were discussing some mundane topic. He appeared the exact opposite of the exposed panic thrashing around Grant's chest at the moment. "Maybe the timing of this is good. I'm glad you asked to meet, actually. Things are getting...weird down at the department."

The exposed panic turned to a cold sense of dread. "Weird how?"

"Well, Internal Affairs was all over us for a couple of days. Not outright, but quietly. A few questions, some top guys showing up for meetings, going over files, that sort of thing."

The satisfaction of knowing his suspicions were being investigated warred with the burden of them being right. Things were on the verge of being exposed. That was good. That was also dangerous. "But..."

"Then poof." Luke spread his fingers. "Everything stops. Like it never happened."

Grant followed his thinking. "Like someone put a stop to it."

Luke nodded. "It'd have to be somebody way up the chain to do that. No one's talking. No one's even admitting that anything happened. Or might have happened. Or even could have happened."

Grant ground his teeth. Why had he even suspected things would come out any other way? Dirty cops with power made for nasty enemies.

"And as for scapegoats, well, you're in the crosshairs."

Of course. Grant could just hear the quietly injected comments. "Let me guess. Guy with anger issues hurls baseless accusations?"

Luke put his fork down. "I know you want to come back, but I don't think you should. They'll be waiting for you. And it won't be with a welcome mat. I know you're dying to yank it all out in the open, but I'm not so sure it's a good idea. I think you should stay away as long as you can manage it. Atkins doesn't want you to come anytime soon." Luke leveled a glare at Grant. "I'm not sure Atkins wants you to come back at all."

That was a chilling thought. "He's either saving me from having to stick my neck out or keeping me out of the way while he covers his tracks." Either way made heading back to Billings an even riskier option.

"No way to know which," Luke said. "Good thing is, no one at the department knows you're in High Mountain. So I think you gotta keep it that way for a while. Till we know more. Till this shakes out."

Grant hated to agree, but he did. "Come on, Mullins, you and I both know things like this don't just 'shake out.'"

Much as Grant hated to admit it, Luke was right. Distance, while aggravating, was the best tactic. This whole thing wasn't going to shake out. It was more likely to explode—and take a lot of people out with it when it did.

Meg relished the silence the next morning. With the girls finally off to school and a spare hour before she had to be at the diner, she needed the solitude to untangle her thoughts. Normally she liked to do that on the porch rocker, but today she felt drawn to the barn. She craved the joyful antics of the puppies. They represented a happy ending of sorts to her—a collection of precious little lives that had been pulled out of danger and into a place where they'd always be loved.

Usually she'd just sit on the hay bales and watch Tabitha and Sadie play with the puppies. Today, she decided to get down on their level and sit in the middle of the pen. It was a good choice—within minutes she was surrounded by love and licks and puppy snuggles. It was simply impossible to keep a smile off her face with all that around her.

"Do you know how you've been blessed?" she asked Licorice, named for his pair of soft black ears. "You're going to have the most wonderful life here. Safe and loved."

The choice of words pricked her heart. She'd been making do and getting by for so long since

Andy died. She always answered "fine" to the dozens of "How are you?"'s—and she was.

Only "fine" wasn't wonderful. It wasn't thriving. It wasn't safe and loved.

I miss feeling safe and loved. It was okay to admit that to God, wasn't it? Pouring her deepest needs out to the Almighty wasn't complaining. It was trusting Him with her honesty.

Daisy limped over to join the pack. The little runt slept without her wheels at night for comfort, and for some reason she didn't have them on yet this morning. "You're not quite the same dog without them, are you? You're just limping along, bless your heart."

Just like me. She was limping along in so many ways. Moving, but capable of so much more. She'd watched Grant and Cay strap the device on Daisy. It didn't seem that difficult. Still, for all Daisy's determination, she needed someone else to put it on.

Meg stood up and crossed the pen to the small shelf where Daisy's canine wheelchair was kept when she wasn't using it. Daisy seemed to know what was coming and waited with a happy little yip for Meg to come back over with the wheels. "Okay, little lady, let me help you get those wheels on."

Let me help you. Wasn't it just like God to speak to her with her own words?

As Meg tucked Daisy's back legs into the device, she was sure the dog looked up to her with grateful eyes. She was eager to let Meg help her. Could she ever say the same of herself? It was okay—welcome, even—for Daisy to accept help for what she couldn't do on her own. Meg had never welcomed help. Most times, she refused it. Help meant dependence, and she had to be strong and independent for her girls.

But did she? What if help meant...help? Care and friendship. Sure, one way to fight the battle of the "not enoughs" was the generosity she'd shown with Hot Dogs for Dogs. And despite Grant's chiding over the logical impracticality of it, Meg knew it was the right choice for her.

But perhaps it wasn't the only choice.

As Meg watched Daisy's joy at zooming around the pen, she sat back and absorbed the lesson being sent to her this morning. "You're just fine with those wheels, aren't you?" she asked the dog. And when Bernard started up a game with his newly mobile littermate, there was no problem. All her littermates accepted Daisy's need for the helping device because the wheels let Daisy be the dog she ought to be. "You all know what I've forgotten," Meg declared to the litter. "Help is a good thing."

Still, help wasn't love. And she missed feeling safe and loved. She was loved in the church

way, in the community way, but not in the soul-
to-soul way she'd once had with Andy. And even
then, she'd felt loved but not always safe. Because Andy was not always safe; his job came
with risk. When had she come to think help
came with a risk?

Daisy rolled up and put her head on Meg's leg
as if to say *You've had it all wrong for a while.*

"I need help." It was surprisingly hard to
admit that out loud, even to a room full of puppies. "I need to accept help. To receive it with the
care people mean by it." The raw, honest words
caught thick in her throat, and Meg found herself wiping away a tear or two—until Licorice
bounded up and tried to lick them off her cheek.

The resulting laughter felt so healing. "You
all are a pretty smart bunch of dogs, you know
that? I might not have caught on if I'd stayed up
on the porch rocking chair."

She made a choice there and then. When help
came, she'd try to open her heart to receive it.
She might even go looking for help. It had to be
out there. Business loans, an easier payment plan
with the mortgage company, perhaps talking
with the bank or her accountant about what to
do. It would sting a bit to admit how bad things
had gotten, but it would sting far more if she let
things go into crisis mode.

This is so hard to do alone. She could find her

way to safe, perhaps, but one person can't find their way to love. It takes two hearts. A rebellious part of her heart yearned for the safety and protection of a man like Grant. In truth, there wasn't much Grant could do to solve her financial troubles. He wasn't rolling in spare money.

But he was all about safety and protection. She could feel his commitment to justice and safety—it was as if the man could have no other profession than law enforcement. Hadn't he said, "I don't live here, and I do what I do for a living"?

"There's not a device in the world that can take away the risk in that," she whispered into Licorice's soft ears. "God's going to have to send my help through some other way."

Still, if God knew her heart—and she was sure He did—He'd know that too much of her yearned for that *safe and loved* feeling to come from the one man she knew couldn't give it.

Chapter Fifteen

Meg hit the switch on the wall that turned off the neon "Open" sign in the diner's front window and waved goodbye to Mike as he left by the back door the next afternoon. She was just reaching for the overhead lights switch when she caught sight of Grant standing outside the front door.

After the way he'd fled the barn the other day, she was surprised to see him. He looked more tense. Worried. He'd said something about needing to meet someone when he'd rushed out, and it wasn't hard to guess that whomever he had met had not brought good news.

She checked her watch, calculated that she had a full twenty minutes before she had to pick the girls up from their church swimming party and waved him inside.

I'd do that for any friend, she reassured herself as he eased onto his customary middle stool.

"I don't suppose you have any cake left?" His words were apologetic—sheepish, almost—as if it was some form of weakness to love her excellent cake.

"As a matter of fact, I do." She drained the last of the coffee into his mug and set it in front of him. "Give me a minute."

It was unwise to be glad there was no one else in the diner. Still, Meg was so aware of the change in his demeanor that she couldn't help but be grateful for the privacy. *Whatever it is, Lord, show me how to help.*

She returned to the counter with a slice of chocolate cake for Grant and a glass of lemonade for herself. "Smile maintenance?" she teased as she set the plate in front of him.

"Something like that," he admitted.

"Cay?"

Grant shook his head. "No. It's work stuff."

Meg settled herself against the counter. "I thought you were on vacation."

"Sometimes work follows you home." His shoulders fell. "Sometimes it follows you everywhere."

"Want to talk about it?" He'd told her only a little bit, and she'd gotten the impression even that was something rare for him.

Grant took a big gulp of coffee, and she glowed a bit inside at the look of deep appreciation on his face. Coffee seemed to mean a lot to him—lots of her customers were like that about their morning brew—and she liked being able to give him this small pleasure.

"One of the worst parts of my job," he began in a weary voice, "is that I usually can't talk about the worst parts."

"Ah, the secret stuff." Andy had a more important-sounding name for it, and for him it was usually the most exciting stuff he couldn't share. "Must be hard not to be able to unburden yourself of the tough stuff."

He gave a small, dark laugh at her choice of words. "Unburden?"

"You have to share the heavy loads. It's too much, otherwise. Even the Bible says that."

She watched his reaction to her bringing up scripture. It wasn't offense that showed on his face—it was more curiosity. Skeptical, but curious. "How do you square that?" he asked.

Order up, Meg said in the silence of her mind. It was her term for when God sent someone into the diner for something other than food. Sure, they ordered, and she fed them, but every once in a while it became crystal clear they'd come in for what Cay would surely call a divine appointment. What would Cay think to know her own son was in the Sundial right now for just such an appointment?

"How so?" It was her favorite way to get someone to tell her more about their thoughts.

"All the Bible stuff. How do you square it with the kind of world we live in?"

It was a surprising question to hear from someone raised by Cay Emerson. He had to have grown up in a home steeped in faith. When had it left him—or he left it?

"Well," she began carefully, "I expect it is harder in the kind of world you live in now. The things you see. But near as I can tell, you can find bad anywhere you are if you look hard enough. Same is true for good. I guess I think of faith as the way you open your eyes to the good. Kindness, grace, forgiveness, that sort of thing. All those can live in even the worst of worlds." She hadn't meant to give such a speech.

He was trying to understand—and genuinely wanted to, from the looks of it. "But all the unfairness. The places where justice just…disappears…if it was ever there in the first place. Where's that God of yours when terrible men gain power and do awful things? When really good people and little girls have to know their husband or dad went down in a plane crash?"

He spoke so pointedly of her loss that it took a moment for her to answer. She knew it would be an important one. "Grant," she said softly, feeling his name echo in her, "God didn't leave me when Andy did. To tell you the truth, He stayed closer than ever. I couldn't have made it through all this without Him. God shows up most of all when things seem worst."

Emboldened by the way he took in her words, she asked, "Are you there? That place where things feel worst?" It had to be something deep and hard. Whatever had made him put a hole in that wall. Whatever had broken that smile.

Grant balked. "How am I supposed to answer a question like that?"

His tone told her how close to home she'd hit. God never wasted one of His divine appointments, and *Order up!* was as much a prayer for the right words as it was a declaration. "The truth, I suppose."

"The truth?" He glared into his coffee for a moment before looking up to meet her eyes. She saw so much pain and anger there that if she didn't know him as well as she did, there might be reason to be afraid. After all, Grant Emerson was a dark and powerful man. Still, she had seen the gentler side of him. The one he tried hard to hide from the world. The side Tabitha and Sadie could bring out so effortlessly in him.

"Yes. If you want." She doubted the wisdom of her bravery for a second but stuck with it. God was never wrong when He sent someone to her counter.

He didn't answer for a while. The clock was

ticking on her picking up the girls, but this wasn't a moment to miss.

He still hadn't touched the cake. "Something awful is happening back in Billings. I'm ticked off. It's bad, it's just going to get worse and I don't think I can stop it. The whole thing is burning in my gut."

"I think God gets that. I think we frustrate Him. You're talking about a God who has watched us down here muck things up over and over. Our free will serves up lots of reasons for us to disappoint the Almighty. I expect I disappoint Him all the time."

"You?" Admiration took away some of the dark in his eyes.

"Like you wouldn't believe. And I'll tell you something, Grant Emerson. It's okay if you disappoint Him, too."

He pulled back. "He's not even looking at me. Where's He looking when the stuff happens that I see?" He thumped his hand on his own broad chest. "*I'm* looking. *I* see it. Doesn't He care about where all the justice went? How guys with all the power get away with stuff? Stuff I'm powerless to stop?"

Grant had such a fierce passion for justice. How could he be anywhere else than law enforcement? She realized, at that moment, that some tiny part of her hoped maybe he could

do something else. That he could stay in High
Mountain. It would give them a wisp of hope for
being together. The power of his words told her
that hope didn't exist. And that was something
she was powerless to change. For the first time,
Meg admitted to herself what a loss that was.

But she could still help him, here and now at
least. "God *is* there," she insisted. "In all that.
I think He sends people like you into a broken
world because you'll fight for people who can't."

"But I can't win," he nearly shouted back.

"Just because you can't win isn't a reason
not to fight. God loves an underdog and a lost
cause. The girls love Daisy more because she
can't run without her wheels. The world handed
those puppies a terrible hand at first, but I know
God also sent Cay. And Vicky. And the pink
wheels. And you."

He wanted to believe that; Meg could see it
in his eyes. "It's not the same. It's not anything
like that."

"It is. Grace is grace in any size you get it.
That's the whole point." Meg's heart sank as
the alarm on her phone went off, telling her it
was time to pick up the girls. Whatever she'd
given Grant today, she would have to trust that
it was enough. It didn't seem like it was. He still
looked like there was nowhere to share his burden, heavy as it was.

"Let me box that cake up for you. You hardly touched it." In fact, he hadn't touched it at all. Meg took out a container before he had the chance to object.

Grant reached for his wallet. "What do I owe you?"

She waved him off. "Nothing. It's on the house."

"Stop doing that," he said. "Stop giving away things to me."

She smiled and snapped the box shut. "Now who's getting frustrated with someone else's free will? Take the cake. And take the sign back to your mom's farm and set it up. We're all waiting on it."

Grant opened his mouth to respond, shut it in frustration, tried again, and finally huffed off to grab the farm sign and begin sliding it toward the door.

"You forgot your cake!" she called after him. The man was infuriating.

Meg's victorious grin as Grant crossed the lawn that evening was amusing. "You came." She said it as if his acceptance of her Please come get your cake text had ever been in question.

Which, of course, it wasn't. He was growing increasingly incapable of missing opportunities to be with her. "It's good cake," he admitted.

"And given that I basically huffed off at the end of our last two conversations… Well, my mama raised me better. And there's these." He held up the small stack of papers he was holding. He'd told himself their delivery was his excuse to see her, but even he didn't believe that.

"What are those?"

The truth was that he'd been so unnerved by their last conversation and so frustrated by his inability to do anything about Billings that he had to find someplace to put all that energy. Rather than admit to all that, he chose a simple term. "Help."

He watched the word hit her as if it had some special meaning. Which it couldn't, since he hadn't explained what he was holding. "Help?" she asked almost shakily.

"Yeah. I needed something to do, so I went on a hunt of sorts. A friend of mine runs an entrepreneurial program in Denver. I contacted him and asked him where a struggling small business in this state run by a veteran family might get some financial help."

When she looked startled, Grant realized he might have crossed a line he shouldn't have crossed. "I never used names or any information. Just asked for websites and that sort of thing. Turns out, there are a bunch of places that can help take the pressure off you."

Meg set the cake box down and leaned against the porch pillar. "You did that?"

Maybe he needed to apologize. She hadn't asked for his help, after all. "I'm sorry. Was that not okay?"

"I don't know." She seemed stunned. It was just a handful of printouts, not the huge thing she seemed to consider it. "You looked for help? For me?"

"I'm sorry. I guess that's meddling. And after all my griping about Mom..." He held out the stack to her, feeling like there was such a huge distance between them. How was it possible to feel so close to her and so far away at the same time?

Meg took it. With both hands. That seemed important somehow. "Thank you," she said in that soft voice that always went right through him. She swallowed hard. "Do you remember how this afternoon I said God shows up most of all when things seem worst?"

"Yeah."

She sank down on the porch steps not two feet away from him. "An hour ago I was adding up bills, wondering how I was ever going to make this work without some help. A day ago I sat in that barn, listening to God tell me I'd better learn how to accept help. I promised Him I would accept the next time someone offered me help. And here you come walking across that field with a stack of it. You used that exact word. *Help*. Don't you tell me that's a coincidence, mister."

He shifted his weight, uncomfortable with what she was implying. He was just a guy trying to kill time, not some agent of divine intervention. "I don't really know if it's help. It's just a list of agencies and applications and stuff."

Meg pulled in a big breath. "Why are you so opposed to being an answer to prayer, Grant?"

"I'm not any kind of answer." The notion of it made his insides twist.

"You are."

"But I'm not that kind of person." He started to say he didn't believe that kind of thing anymore, but he couldn't. Some rebellious part of him was starting to believe again. There was too much evidence for his cop brain to ignore it.

"You don't have to be any kind of person. Because He's every kind of God. Which makes you, Grant Emerson, an answer to prayer." One corner of her mouth twisted up into an adorably defiant grin. "And not for the first time, I might add."

Why was he always doing battle with the urge to run from and the pull to stay near this woman? "I should go." He nodded toward the papers. "I hope there's something useful in there."

She held the ordinary printouts with tender

care. As if they were a gift. Maybe they were. A peace offering, if nothing else. The measly gesture of a man who wanted to help her but had no real idea how.

"I know there is," she replied. "And I will accept this help because I know God sent it. Through you."

She had a talent for saying things that tangled him up inside. He took a step back, feeling more unsteady by the minute. "I should go."

"Not before you take your cake," she commanded. "Don't you dare walk across that field without your cake."

He couldn't have refused for all the world.

It was Meg, after all. And it was very good cake.

Chapter Sixteen

❧

Mom seemed to have invited half the town of High Mountain to watch the Three Sisters Rescue Farm sign being raised, and it seemed all of them came.

Grant had hoped to work without fanfare, but he should have known better. Mom had set out picnic tables and pitchers of lemonade. Aunt Barb and Aunt Peggy brought enough cookies to feed the entire county. Sinking a post in the ground, mixing cement and raising the sign couldn't possibly be as entertaining as the sisters made it out to be. While it was a sunny morning, the fact that it had rained late last night left the ground soggy in places, making his job harder. If he ended up with a sign that tilted to the side like the Tower of Pisa, Grant was sure he'd never hear the end of it.

"Hope you're not expecting me to provide color commentary," he said to his mother as he laid out the shovel, post-hole digger and other tools on the ground beside the spot she'd picked out.

Mom beamed. "You just get that gorgeous hunk of wood up and I'll do the rest." She gazed at the sign as if it were a precious thing. Maybe to her, it was. She'd been harboring this dream for far longer than he realized, and the sign seemed to announce it to the world.

On impulse, Grant handed the shovel to her. "How about you do the honors? First dig and all." It was, after all, akin to a groundbreaking ceremony like he'd seen down at Billings City Hall. This was Mom's big day, and despite his misgivings, she ought to have it.

Her smile widened. "I think I'd like that." Raising her voice, she called out, "Gather round, everyone. Here goes!"

With nothing short of glee, Mom sank the blade of the shovel into the ground. Everyone cheered. Sadie and Tabitha jumped up and down, whooping and clapping their hands.

The first shovelful achieved, Mom gestured to her sisters. "Each of you, too." Peggy, then Barb, dug up a bit more as the cheers continued.

Mom handed the shovel back to Grant after the ceremonial digging. "The rest is up to you, son."

"We'll need a few hands when it's time to raise it up," he said.

Mom glanced around. "Why do you think I invited all these people?"

Grant knew better. "You invited them all because you wanted to throw a big party for your sign."

Her grin couldn't help but warm a corner of Grant's heart. "Well, that, too. Everybody wins."

Her comment recalled Grant's frustrated drive back from the diner and his meeting with Luke. It didn't feel like he lived in a world where everybody wins. In truth, his world lately felt like a place where most people lost.

Except for here. He'd felt trapped here after Luke's admonition to still stay away from Billings. But today actually felt good. A counterbalance to everything else in his life. Mom and Meg kept calling him an answer to prayer. He couldn't quite get his head around that, but a small part of his heart seemed to be toeing up the idea.

Grant was just picking up the post-hole digger—a heavy two-handled, two-bladed contraption meant to dig deep and narrow—when Tabitha walked up. "Can I help?"

The implement was taller than she was, and hefty even for a man of his size. Still, Grant found he couldn't deny the girl the chance to help. But how?

Hitting on an idea, he said, "Sure, but it'll take both your sister and you."

"Okay." With that, Tabitha darted off to find Sadie while Grant maneuvered the digger into the hole begun by his mother and aunts. The rain had softened the ground just enough that he might be able to pull this off.

Meg returned with the girls. "Going to let them help, are you?"

"Just a bit," he teased. There was something about the warmth in her eyes that he was sure would stay with him long after he could finally return to Billings. Confound it, Luke was right. He had fallen for her. And the girls. For a man who saw too much of how unfair the world was, that fact pierced him as doubly unfair. Wouldn't you know it that when he finally did fall for someone, it was someone he never ought to have.

"What do we do?" Sadie asked.

"You see these two handles here? Lucky for me, I have two helpers. So each of you, grab on to the handles here." He pointed to a spot just over halfway up the long broomstick-like handles of the digger.

The girls quickly positioned themselves on either handle. Grant held the handles farther up, both to keep the implement upright and to provide a little assistance. "Ready?"

"Ready!" the girls chimed in unison, faces fixed in serious expressions.

"Now, when I say, you both pull as hard as you can. Got it?" He caught Meg's charmed smile out of the corner of his eye and decided that maybe, today, everybody did win.

"Got it." The girls adjusted their stance, ready to pull with all their little mights.

"Pull!"

The girls yanked with surprising force, sending both of the digger's blades toward each other inside the hole. The process cut a plug of sorts out of the dirt. "Okay, let's see what we got."

The girls released their grip, and Grant pulled the digger up out of the hole. "Well, will you look at that?" he marveled to the small clod of dirt sitting between the blades. It was as if the playful tone of his voice was coming out of some strange Grant he'd never been. "That's a fine bit of digging."

"Can we do it again?" Tabitha asked eagerly.

They ended up doing it four times until the girls pleaded that they were too tired to do more. In truth, Grant could have done the whole thing in three strokes, if not less. But it was too much fun to let the girls feel as if they'd helped. Somehow the heavy digger felt that much lighter as he sank it into the ground enough times to create a hole deep enough to support the sign.

Meg walked up to him with a glass of lemonade when he finally laid the digger down. "That was sweet of you."

Grant laughed as he accepted the cold drink.

"Pretty sure no one's ever said that to me before."

"I love that they'll look out our window at the sign and know they helped put it up there. Thanks for that gift."

Grant was sure his neck was reddening, and it had nothing to do with his recent exertion. "Mom's doing, really."

"Nope," she refuted. "That one's all you."

"I just let them hold the handles."

She gave him one of *those* looks, the *Don't think you're going to get away with that* glare. On Mom, a look like that annoyed him. On Meg, it just dug under his skin in the best of ways.

"You and I both know it was more than that. Why is it so hard for you to believe you're one of the good guys? You have to know the girls adore you."

"They adore the puppies," he countered.

"You, too. We don't make cake for just anybody, you know."

He gulped down the last of the lemonade rather than admit to the way her voice made him feel. "Okay then, I'd better go get this sign vertical, or Mom'll be after me."

"For a guy itching to leave, you've done a lot of good around here," Meg reminded him as she took the empty lemonade glass from him.

He knew she wasn't just talking about the sign.

* * *

When the signpost sank into the hole, it made a satisfying thunk Meg was sure she felt in her bones. Every single person erupted in cheers, as if they'd planted a flag on the moon. The girls squealed and did a silly dance around Grant as he nailed a trio of support two-by-fours in place to keep the sign straight when he poured the cement into the hole.

Cay pulled Meg into a hug as they took in the glory of the posted sign a few minutes later. "Will you look at that?"

"It's beautiful," Meg agreed. "You can see it for half a mile down the road in either direction, I expect."

"Declaring Three Sisters Rescue Farm to the world." The woman's joy was contagious.

A question struck her. "What will you do if someone leaves a basket of kittens under the sign?"

Meg shouldn't have been surprised when Cay replied, "Already thought of that. Peggy's building me a little wooden box that will have a sheet of instructions inside telling folks what to do if they have an animal for the farm. And someone from church is going to build us a website where you can apply to bring your animals or donate."

Everything about the farm pulled at Meg in a way she couldn't explain. One thing she knew for certain; she would fight with all she had to keep this land from the fate of so many local family farms. Three Sisters Rescue Farm could never become a subdivision or some other common batch of homes. It was too special to ever be anything but what it was about to become. What it already had become.

A shriek interrupted their conversation, and the whole crowd turned to see the cause. Meg gasped as she saw a stampede of puppies scattering across the field in all directions.

A suspicion almost made her shriek herself, and Meg scanned the crowd for the whereabouts of her daughters. They weren't here, which could only mean…

Sure enough, Tabitha and Sadie emerged from the huge barn opening. They ran after one puppy and then another, but even Daisy and her wheels were too fast. Within seconds, puppies were everywhere.

"They're out!" Peggy yelled, starting toward the canine chaos.

"And we don't have a gate yet!" Barb added. "Catch them!"

Everyone began heading toward a puppy, hoping to corral them before any of the dogs made it through the gate and onto the road. The puppies were bigger now, however, and catching them proved far from easy.

"I'm sorry, Mama!" Tabitha wailed as Meg ran up beside her and they headed behind Daisy, who took off past the house. Grant had paired up with Sadie and gone after two others. "They wanted to see the sign."

Meg kept running with Tabitha in tow. "Of course they did, sweetheart, but they're too young to go out without a leash. And the gate is gone."

The girls clearly hadn't thought about that. Tabitha stopped running as worry filled her face. "No gate. They'll run away." She began to cry.

"Not if we catch them first," Meg replied, grabbing Tabitha's hand. "There's lots of us and only eight of them. We'll fix this."

"We gotta," Tabitha moaned. "Come back, Daisy!"

They both began calling Daisy, hoping to lure her back from her escapade. But Daisy, like the other pups, was delighted to get the chance to run wherever she wanted. None of them were in any hurry to come when called.

"Barb!" Meg heard Cay call from behind her. "There's chicken in the fridge. Bring some out here to lure them back."

While Meg wasn't sure even Cay's best roasted chicken could compete with a chance to roam free over the farm fields, it was worth a shot. At least none of them had headed toward the sign, as far as she could tell. There wasn't much traffic along the road that passed the farm, but if one of those little darlings got out and came to harm... She didn't want to consider that terrible possibility.

Daisy rolled clear around the house, still faster on her two wheels than Meg or Tabitha. As they came around back to the open field, Meg spied Luther Beckham, the town fire chief, making a spectacular leap to grab one of the puppies just beyond a line of bushes. "Got 'em!" he cried as he clamped a grip on the wriggling animal. Peggy, who had wisely headed into the barn and grabbed the eight leashes hanging there—why hadn't the girls thought to use the leashes?— rushed to Luther and snapped one on the dog.

The next twenty minutes became a wild game of Catch the Puppy, with all manner of strategies being put in play. Mike the cook tried coaxing one over with a stick to play fetch. Pastor Jim snuck up on one taking a breather under the porch and snapped a leash on before the dog knew she'd been captured. One by one, the puppies were captured and brought to safety, with Daisy eluding everyone almost until the end.

"One, two, three, four, five, six," Cay counted, nearly out of breath. "Where's the last two?"

Meg looked around and realized neither Grant nor Sadie were anywhere in sight. She hoped that didn't spell disaster.

Peggy, still holding the last two leashes, pointed beyond a bale of hay in the side field. "There they are!"

Walking toward the crowd were the silhouettes of a large man holding a small girl...and two barking dogs at either end of a rope. Grant had Sadie in his arms. She had her tiny head buried into his broad shoulder, and the sight sank straight into Meg's heart.

She started walking toward the pair and quickly realized what she hadn't seen before. Grant and Sadie were covered in mud. In fact, it was hard to say who had more mud on them—the puppies or the people. Somehow that made the scene all the more sweet.

"I'm sorry, Mama. I ruined the puppies and my dress. I ruined everything."

There was something so tender in the firm hold Grant had on Sadie. "You didn't ruin anything, honey," Meg consoled her. "All the puppies are safe and sound."

"I fell in the mud. I'm all muddy."

"We're both muddy," Grant admitted, handing the makeshift leash off to Cay, who had dashed up behind them at admirable speed.

"I can see that," Cay said.

"I ruined my dress," Sadie repeated, picking at the soaked skirt that now stuck to her legs.

"It'll come out in the wash. Everyone's safe.

That's what matters." Meg held out her arms for her daughter.

"I'll hang on to her," Grant said. "No need for everyone to get muddy." He reached up his now-free hand and wiped a smear of mud from his chin. How had he gotten so dirty so quickly?

"How did everyone get muddy?" she asked.

Sadie sniffled. "I fell and Mr. Grant came in after me."

Meg raised an eyebrow at Grant in question. "You jumped in a giant mud puddle after my daughter and the puppies?"

"Pretty much how it happened," he replied.

Sadie looked up at Grant with an expression of hero-worship. "You saved me," she pronounced with great drama.

"Nah," he said. "Pretty much saved each other. And then we both saved the puppies. No harm done, right, Sadie girl?"

Affection. The affection Grant had for Sadie glowed bright under all the mud.

"That's my Grant," Cay declared. "The man saves people like he breathes air."

"Mama," Sadie began in a small, pitiful voice, "Mr. Grant's mama isn't mad at him for being muddy. Are you mad at me?"

The clever question made Grant grin. And then chuckle. And then the man broke into a full laugh with a broad smile.

Meg had been wondering if the man would be especially handsome if he ever really fully smiled.

Now she knew the answer.

Chapter Seventeen

It took forever to get the girls settled down for bed that night. They were both rattled by what had happened and wound up from all the excitement. They bounced back and forth between being victorious about the puppy rescue and guilt-ridden over their escape.

Thank You, Lord, that everyone is safe, Meg prayed as she eased her tired body into the porch rocking chair. The light was fading over the fields, and the silhouette of the new sign stood tall against the golden streaks of the setting sun. What a day this had been. For that matter, what a week and month it had been. For all the chaos, it still felt good to feel something other than weary endurance.

And she *was* feeling things. After this afternoon, Meg could no longer deny how hard she was falling for Grant. That stack of help in her desk drawer drew her like the most romantic of poems. It felt as if God had sent them. It felt as if

God had sent him. *You know this is impossible, Lord*, she lamented. *He's a police officer. He's in Billings. I can't do that to my heart or my girls.*

None of that stopped her heart from the unwise hope that she would see the silhouette of one tall man walking across the field. Meg told herself it was because she wanted to thank him, but she'd already thanked him multiple times. The girls had thanked him endlessly.

No, the sense of longing welling up inside her had nothing to do with gratitude. Now gratitude was only a small part of it. The other parts were stronger and, quite frankly, more unsettling.

She had begun to wonder what she would do if Grant had acted on what she saw in his eyes. If he took her hand or took her in his arms. There wasn't much wondering to it—she would melt into the strength of his embrace.

She found herself in a precarious place, feeling fragile and vibrant all at the same time. She was stepping out of the long shadow of grief and struggle. *How long have I wondered what it would feel like to rise up out of all that grief? But him? Now? You've got to protect me, Lord. I'm pretty sure I can't do it myself.*

She couldn't make herself go back inside. Some stubborn part of her would sit here on the porch and wait for Grant to walk across the field. And so Meg couldn't say if it was minutes or hours before, in the last light of the day, she saw Grant's figure making his way toward the porch. It worried her how her pulse jumped as he stood at the bottom of her stairs. He hesitated just off her porch. She did not move from her spot on the chair. Did he also feel that taking that step might mean crossing a line?

He'd cleaned himself up from the muddy mess of earlier. How telling, she thought to herself, that she found him doubly handsome covered in mud and holding Sadie tightly. Still, there was no question the man cleaned up nicely. Framed in the light coming from the house, he cut a ruggedly dashing figure. She couldn't say if it was her imagination—or even wishful thinking—that his face had softened. Much of the continual frown he'd worn when they'd first met was gone. And that laugh she'd finally heard? That full smile? Well, it would be a long time before she forgot that sound and sight, if ever.

He gave an almost boyish grin. "Some day, huh?"

"The girls were riled up for hours. I only just got them to bed."

He leaned against the porch pillar. "Are they okay? They know Mom isn't mad at them, don't they?"

"Let's just say, I think Tabitha and Sadie will

be extra careful with the puppies from now on. That's not a bad thing."

Grant put one foot on the bottom stair. "Let's all just be happy it was just puppies, not any of the other animals Mom might think about taking in. She said something the other day about miniature pigs, and imagine how that would have played out."

"Muddier?" she joked. It came out more nervous than funny.

He tried to laugh, but it had the same tightness she felt in her chest. So much seemed to be echoing in the air between them that small talk felt almost impossible.

She made herself go deeper. "I keep trying to think of ways to thank you for what you did today. It means a lot to me."

He looked at his shoes. "You already said *thanks*. I think about eight times." He brought his gaze back up again. "It's nothing. I like them. They only meant well and wanted to help and they're just so…sweet." It was as if the last word pushed itself out of him against his will.

"They like you, too," she replied. *I like you. Rather a lot. What on earth am I supposed to do with that?* "Sadie actually said the words 'He's my hero' tonight."

Grant grinned and flushed. The charm of his

reaction went straight through her. "Oh, I don't know that I'm anybody's hero."

"I imagine there are quite a few people in Billings who would argue with that. Maybe even a few right here in High Mountain."

"Mom doesn't count," he teased.

"Moms absolutely do count," she teased back. Feeling braver for the light banter, Meg stood up and walked to the railing. She had to hold on to it, the dizzying effect of the sunset and Grant's nearness playing games with her.

Grant walked up the stairs. He didn't mount the last step—the one that would put him on the porch with her—but it did place him much closer. He pivoted to follow Meg's gaze out over the fields. "I forgot just how pretty this place is. And how quiet."

"Most of the time I love it," she admitted. "Sometimes it feels lonely, but the wide open space is comforting, too."

"Are you? Lonely?" He spoke the words so softly she barely heard him.

Meg found she couldn't lie. Not to him. Not now. "Sometimes." It only seemed right to ask him, "Are you?"

"All the time," he answered with heartbreaking simplicity.

"That's awful," she said, fighting the urge to put a hand on his arm. He was close enough. She could reach out easily. But she would be crossing so much more than just the space between them.

He shook his head and stepped up onto the porch. "Nah. I've been alone for so long I don't even recognize it anymore. Used to, at least."

Used to. She recognized his use of the past tense. Her pulse felt like it was rushing through her, a once-quiet stream now roaring over its banks. "What changed?"

Grant didn't say anything. He just looked at her, the sad wonder in his eyes saying everything.

"Must have been some cake," she deflected, needing some escape from the way he was making her feel.

"No cake," he said. He wasn't going to let her evade this, and that terrified her. He walked over and stood next to her. The world tilted a bit, and Meg gripped the porch rail.

He looked down, noticing her white-knuckled grip on the wood. Grant put his hand on top of hers. It was warm and broad, roughened a bit from the day's work of putting up the sign. She felt her resistance giving way, despite every attempt to keep it in place.

"I want you to know," he said in a low, surprisingly gentle voice, "how I wish there was a chance for something here. I never in a million years expected it. If things were different…"

"Things aren't different." There was so much regret piled up behind those words that Meg's throat tightened with the threat of tears.

"No." Still, he did not remove his hand from hers.

That one small word weighed a million pounds.

"I am going to miss the girls when I go back to Billings. I'm going to… I'm going to miss you."

"But you *are* going back to Billings. Back to the police department and everything that means." She had to put that into words, to declare it and hope it would fill up the humming air between them.

"I am. I always was." He gave a long sigh. "Not sure when, but I will. I don't know that I've been any help here…"

"You *have*," she insisted. His help went much further than a stack of printouts or a fixed lock or any of the other practical things he'd done. Meg placed her other hand atop his. She knew, with a tinge of both regret and relief, that it would be the closest they would ever come to that embrace. "I hope you know how much we will miss you."

She would miss him. She, with her diner and her girls and all those friends, would miss *him*. It seemed impossible. She was this great big phenomenon in his life, but Grant didn't feel anywhere near special enough to leave a hole in hers. The girls', maybe, but her?

The phrase *I don't deserve you* was so over-used, but it was exactly what was thrumming through his heart right now. Meg should have everything she wanted in a man, a father, a life partner. Sure, with time and her affection, he might be some of those things, but it would never change the basic pieces of who he was. He was a cop. A man who risked his life every day. You couldn't transplant a career like his here to tiny High Mountain. And he didn't know how to do anything else. Wasn't sure he could be happy doing anything else.

Still, Grant knew. He knew the illogical, un-tested, not-a-shred-of-evidence truth that he could be happy with *her*. To come home to those three every night, to watch Tabitha and Sadie grow up? The lure of it pulled at him with so much force he began to doubt his own convictions.

But it was selfish and unreasonable to pull her into his life. Especially now, with what was surely ahead back in Billings. Grant had to shore up those convictions, to protect her by not being with her. The one gift he could give her—if you could call it a gift—was to let her know what it cost him to leave her.

"I will miss you," he repeated, giving weight to each word. "If there was some way…"

Meg's eyes glistened, and Grant silently begged her not to cry. If she cried, he was sure he would lose the battle to take her into his arms, and then it would all be hopeless.

"The worst part is…," she began in a forced brightness that near broke his heart, "there is no way."

The words pounded into him. Dull, because he'd known that all along, and yet sharp because it hurt so much to hear her speak them. To him. About him.

"I wouldn't trade today for the world." For everything else that would never be, they still did have today. Mud and cheers and the incredible feeling of Sadie's little arms wrapped around his neck. The more incredible feeling of Meg's hands, one still under his and the other still tenderly laid on top.

She smiled even as her eyes glistened. "Me neither. Today will always be special." She pulled herself up a bit. "It's not as if you won't come back. Your mom and aunts are here. Somebody's going to have to try to talk a bit of sense into Cay now and then. It'll be fine."

Meg said that last bit with no conviction whatsoever. Grant realized there was a dose of heartbreak in this for her as well. His would be for a long time—maybe always. Hers would fade, because Meg couldn't help but love. Someone would come into her life and give her all she ought to have. This time would become a bittersweet memory, a "remember that spring?" conversation as the girls grew older.

Recklessly, Grant moved his hands so that they now wrapped around hers. "Thank you for fixing my smile. For...all the things you've done."

His tone seemed to startle her, widening her eyes. "You're talking like it's all over. You're not leaving yet...are you?"

Grant took a tiny bit of satisfaction from her reluctance to let him leave. "Not yet, no. But this part of it has to be over." Not that it ever really started. It couldn't. But that irrational possibility? The one they both hung on to for no good reason? That had to be over.

Meg's expression told him she knew what he was saying, knew the words behind his words. She gave a very slight nod.

There were a million reasons not to do it, but Grant raised her hands and planted a small, quiet kiss on each one. How anything could hurt so much and feel so amazing was beyond him. Painful as it was, he couldn't bring himself to regret it.

Meg gave a soft whimper and leaned a bit toward him.

He pushed back on her hands, stopping her

from coming any closer. He had to be the strength they both needed, to be the protector it was in his bones to be.

Grant should say some perfect thing, some noble words that would let them both know this was the only way things would end. The right man for Meg would do something like that.

But he wasn't the right man for Meg. So, in the end, Grant just let her hands slip from his and dragged himself off the porch into the now-dark night. He forced himself not to look back.

The walk back to the farmhouse was ages long and pitch-black dark.

Chapter Eighteen

"Grant. Grant!" Mom's urgent voice and her hand shaking his shoulder pulled Grant from the fitful sleep he'd finally found near dawn.

Checking the ingrained response to defend himself whenever he was woken up, Grant reminded himself where he was and rolled over. The early morning sun threw a pink-gray light over his mother's worried face. "Huh?"

"Get up. Something's happened."

She looked unharmed, but her hand had a vise grip on his shoulder. The house? The dogs? "What?"

She dashed over to the window as Grant swung his legs out of bed. The combination of alarm and weariness threw him a bit off-balance, and he rubbed his eyes as she pointed out the window.

"The sign," she nearly wailed. "The sign."

"What about the sign?" He followed her to the window. It took him a moment to work out what she meant: the sign wasn't there. Even in the dim sunrise, it should be clearly in view out next to where the gate would be when it was re-placed. It wasn't. "It's sunk in cement. How'd it fall over?" Of all the jobs he knew he had to get right...

"It didn't fall over, son. It was cut down."

Grant was wide awake now. "Cut down?" He reached for the sweatshirt piled on a nearby chair and pulled it on over the sweatpants he was wearing. "You're sure?" He realized his mother had a coat over her nightgown and boots on. She'd gone out there.

"I heard a noise about an hour ago. I just had a bad feeling about it."

He scrambled for his shoes at the foot of the bed. "You didn't get me then?"

"I just... I don't know... I didn't think." She grabbed his hand and met his gaze. "It was axed down. It didn't fall. Someone cut my sign down."

The sign had meant such a victory to her. Yesterday when it had gone up was practically a holiday to her, the official launch of Three Sisters Rescue Farm. Who'd knock something like that down? He stuffed his feet into his shoes. "Let's go look."

When they got to the edge of the drive, Grant found the sign face down in the grass. He'd hoped Mom was overstating things, but she wasn't. Clear axe marks showed where the signpost had been freshly severed. It hadn't been accidentally pushed or been the victim of some random wind burst.

Someone had cut the sign down.

He reached down and turned the heavy sign back over. It was a blessing, he supposed, that the sign was still intact. "Doesn't seem to be any damage," he offered, hoping to soothe Mom's wounded expression.

She reached down and touched the corner as if consoling it. "Who'd do this?"

Vandalism wasn't uncommon on his patrols. Most times it was just kids being thoughtless. Looking for a thrill and not really caring what damage they caused. "Some kids, I expect." While the gate could be a total accident, this had the markings of a prank. "I don't think anyone's out to get the farm."

Even as he spoke the words, however, a small curl of suspicion planted itself in Grant's gut. What had his training sergeant once said? *One incident is an incident. Two could be a pattern. Three is a problem.*

Mom huffed. "Of course no one's out to get the farm. What is it with kids these days? Why do they have to have their fun at someone else's expense?" Her words were defiant, but Grant didn't like the edge of fear she didn't quite hide in her tone.

"If kids behaved like rational adults, half my job would be gone." That wasn't exactly true—he mostly dealt with young men and adults who had gone far beyond the prank phase—but he hoped it would help Mom keep from getting too wound up. She was taking this very personally.

"What do we do?"

She'd said "we." It poked again at that part of Grant that worried how she would cope out here on her own and made him glad Meg and the girls were just a stone's throw away. Peggy and Barb were each a twenty-minute drive away—too far for anything urgent or frightening like this.

"Well," he began as he dragged the sign over to sit upright against the fence, "get that new gate in here, for starters." The sign was inside the fence. While that wasn't a huge deterrent, in Grant's experience kids took the low-hanging fruit on stuff like this. Even the smallest obstacle usually sent them on to something easier.

"I called again to confirm they're coming on Thursday." She tightened her coat around her. For as warm as the weather had been, this morning had a chill to it.

Grant used his sleeve to brush the dirt and grass from the edges of the sign. "You ought to file a police report. This probably is below your insurance deductible, but I can get a metal post from the supply store and remount the sign on that." It seemed sad to have to do it over again without the celebration of yesterday. The vandals probably had no idea that the damage they'd caused went far beyond just an axe and a wooden post.

He turned to head back toward the house, but Mom just stood there, staring at the sign as it leaned lopsidedly on the stub of its former post. "Who'd do this?" she repeated. "Why?"

He wrapped his arm around her and turned her toward the house. "Sometimes there just isn't an answer. You're okay, the sign's okay, the dogs are okay..."

"The dogs!" Mom began trotting toward the barn at high speed. "I didn't check on the dogs. They didn't do anything to the dogs, did they?"

Grant caught up to her. "I don't think they'd head that far onto the property." He had no basis for his assumption. Out of nowhere, he flung a *Let those dogs be safe* toward Heaven as they rushed toward the large barn door and pulled it open. His first prayer in probably a decade, if not more.

"Oh, thank goodness," Mom sighed as they both spied the puppies sound asleep in a furry pile at one corner of the pen. Of course, they didn't stay that way. The sound of the door woke them up, and within half a minute, they were barking and pushing their noses through the fence to greet Mom. Even Daisy wobbled her way over without her wheels to say hello.

The surge of gratitude and relief in Grant's chest caught him off guard. He never expected to become so fond of the little dogs. If he had a different life, he might have even thought about taking one home with him to Billings. Several of the guys on the force had pets, and the department even had a few canine officers handling specially trained dogs.

They retired those police dogs at some point, didn't they? Maybe he could arrange for one to find its way here. If nothing else, the big breed could serve as a deterrent to any more stunts like this. And while Mom would never take on a dog for security purposes, she'd be unlikely to refuse a rescue.

As he stood there watching Mom love on the puppies, cooing about how glad she was that they were safe, Grant's cell phone buzzed in his pocket.

It was a three-word text from the burner phone Luke used to contact him.

Come back. Now.

Meg stared at the broken glass, and then the cell phone in her shaking hand. *Don't call Grant. Call someone else. Call anyone else.*

She should call the police. Or Mike, even though he was due at the diner in half an hour. There were two or three people from church she could call.

She *wanted* to call Grant. In fact, if she were honest, she *needed* to call Grant. The urge to have him near, given the gaping hole in the diner's back window and the twisted metal of the jimmied-open back door, was too strong to resist.

He'd know what to do. He'd know what *not* to do. And while there was probably a handful of people who could give her that information, she wanted to hear it from *him*.

Extenuating circumstances, she told herself as she touched his name on her phone screen.

"Meg," he said after picking up immediately.

"You picked up fast."

"My phone was in my hand. Everything okay?" His tone held both surprise and alarm. It was early in the day to be calling. And given how they'd ended things last night, he had every right to be surprised she'd called.

She allowed herself the luxury of total honesty. "No." Her voice wobbled even on the single syllable. "Something's happened. I need your help."

"The girls?" She was touched by the instant

concern that filled his voice. "Are you or the girls hurt?"

"No, we're okay. I'm at the Sundial. Someone… Someone's busted through the back door and broke the back window."

"You're there? Alone?" She could hear him grabbing his car keys. It was okay that she felt relief knowing he was on his way. This was scary stuff.

"There's no one else here. Whoever did this is long gone."

She could hear him walking fast and pictured him dashing toward his truck. "Are you sure? Have you checked?"

Meg could see every corner of the diner from where she stood. "Yes. Unless he's hiding in the freezer, no one's here." She used to love the quiet of the diner when she was the first to arrive. Now she wondered if she ever would again.

The truck's ignition sounded in the background. "I'm on my way. Did you call the police?"

"No," she admitted. "I called you." She could worry about what that revealed later. Still, she backpedaled. "I mean, you *are* the police, right?"

Grant gave one of his characteristic grunts. "Is the door too broken to lock? Is the front door working and locked?"

"Thanks to you, yes. And I think I can shove the back door into place and throw the deadbolt."

"Do both. And don't touch anything else. I'm on my way."

The clear command in Grant's voice soothed her. This was what he did. Crime and protection were his world, and he would know what to do despite how foreign the situation was to her.

Meg pushed the big metal back door into place, jiggled the deadbolt until it sank home and made her way to the center counter stool. It was as if her legs gave out underneath her, the dark memory of bad news' rush of adrenaline bringing up old feelings. The appearance of men at her door with the news of Andy's fatal crash. The blanked-out "What do I do now?" tangle of thoughts. It wasn't the same level of catastrophe, but her body didn't seem to distinguish between the two events.

Do something. Do anything.

Her hands shook as she turned on the coffee machine, grounds spilling out of the filter. She dashed to the door when she saw Grant's headlights pull up to the sidewalk outside.

Terrible idea or not, she ran straight at Grant and clung to him, nearly knocking him over in the process. He jolted at the sudden contact, but put his arms around her and held tight for the few seconds she allowed him.

It was a small yet enormous moment. For as numb as she seemed to be, Meg felt every detail of the contact. How his breath hitched, how broad his chest was, the roughness of his shirt, the steadiness of his arms. For all the girls' teasing fascination with Grant's sheer size, she was endlessly grateful for it right now.

"Sorry," she gasped out the moment she could gather her composure and pull back. Only she wasn't, really. Embarrassed, caught off guard, maybe, but not sorry.

"Don't be," he said gruffly. He looked as flustered as she felt. Did his arms hesitate just a bit to let her go, or did she imagine it?

"Nothing like this has ever happened to me before. No one's ever keyed my car or broken into it or I've never even had my bicycle stolen as a kid." She was babbling, but it was safer to list that than to voice the huge relief filling her insides at his presence.

Grant took her arm—tenderly, given the man's size—and led her to the counter stools. "It's a scary thing to be a victim."

How had he managed to voice the exact thing she needed to hear? "It is," she replied as she sat down. She'd endured the trauma of Andy's accident, but this morning she was a victim. That's why it felt so different and yet similar at the same time.

He went to the sink and filled a glass of water. "Take a drink."

"I made coffee," she blurted out, pointing to the percolating machine.

His small grin was just the foothold she needed. "Of course you did. In a bit, okay?" He set the glass in front of her. Meg was struck by the irony of him serving her at the counter instead of the other way around. "Drink while I check things out."

Just before he turned toward the back door, Grant caught her gaze. "I'm glad you called me."

Meg was so sure she'd overstepped, that she'd imposed on Grant and the limits they'd set last night. Not that any of such thoughts kept her from the impulse to call him first before the more logical step of dialing the High Mountain Police Department. She nodded, both hands wrapped around the water glass like a small child.

He came back just a few moments later. Grant had what Meg could only describe as "a policeman's expression" on his face. Official, assessing, in control. "Anything missing? The register open, anything like that?"

In her fright, she hadn't even thought to check the register for missing cash. "It's empty. I took a deposit to the bank yesterday, and I have the drawer till with me because I needed more small bills."

Grant walked over to the register. "It hasn't

been opened. I doubt this was a robbery. There's been a run of...." Grant didn't finish the sentence, but his face changed. The calm control evaporated into something else. A cross between dread and anger that sent Meg's pulse rising again.

"What?" she asked.

Grant's eyes squinted shut for a minute, and she noticed his fists tightening. His shoulders tensed, and she could see his jaw clench as he sat down on the stool next to her with deliberate, precise movements.

"What?" she said again, growing fearful at what had come over him.

"This isn't a robbery. It's not vandalism. It's a warning."

Chapter Nineteen

The fear in Meg's eyes was like a stake of ice into Grant's chest. "What on earth do you mean?" she asked warily.

One incident is an incident. Two could be a pattern. Three is a problem.

"The farm gate. The sign. And now this. There's a common denominator here."

How had he blinded himself to seeing it? Why had it taken Luke's text to connect the obvious dots? Had it gone too far and put people he cared about at risk?

He made himself say it, forced himself to give Meg the honesty she deserved. After all, she had called *him*, not the local cops. "Me."

"You?"

A war was going on inside Grant. To tell her might put her at greater risk. But to not tell her was cruel and gave her more reason to fear. This had gone far beyond a simple declaration of "I'll take care of it." She deserved to know what was going on—or what he now was nearly certain was going on.

It took him a minute to find the right words. "Someone is using you—and Mom—to let me know they know where I am." Voicing the thought turned his stomach and lit fire to the anger that he'd been trying so hard to snuff out.

"I don't understand. Who? Why?"

Grant gave in to the impulse to take Meg's hands into his as he had on the porch. "Well, you know I'm not exactly here on vacation."

Meg cocked her head to one side. "I figured it had to be more than just a hole in some office wall. What is this really about?"

How could he explain this very complicated situation without telling Meg more than was safe for her to know? "I put that hole in that wall because I uncovered some dirty stuff going on in my department. Very deep and going very high up." Grant flexed his fingers, remembering the boiling frustration that sent that punch through that wall. "I was ticked off because no one seemed willing to believe me. Or to do anything about it if they did. Because I know, now, that almost everyone who *could* do something about it was involved. Which makes me a liability, not just a guy with a bad temper."

"So they sent you away to get you out of the way?"

Meg was as clever as she was brave. Even now she'd gained her composure back faster than most victims he'd encountered. She was an overcomer. More importantly, she was someone he cared about. How had those lowlifes known she would be the final straw to back him down? "I'm so sorry you got caught up in this," he said, meaning every word. "I can't stay here now that they know where I am. It's time to go back to Billings and fight this out. Stand up against the whole lot of them before they try something else." He almost said *You'll be safer that way*, but he didn't want to give her more reason to fear.

He'd called this all wrong. He should have gone with his first impulse to hermit away in some remote mountain cabin. At least if they came after him there, all this wouldn't have happened.

But he had come here. And in doing so he'd met Meg and the girls. What kind of fool could be thankful for something like that and regret it so deeply at the same time?

"You have to," Meg agreed. "Go back to Billings and find someone who will listen. Find a way to expose whatever this is and fight it."

This was the woman who'd told him her life had been shredded by risk. Now she was asking him to risk more?

No, she was asking him to fight back, to fight

harder. Back in Billings, his frustration at the injustice buried his drive to fight. Plain and simple: he'd let the bad guys win. That surrender was so far against his nature—no wonder he'd felt tied in knots for months.

"There's a fair chance this won't end well. These are powerful people."

"Grant," she said, the way she said his name sinking deep into his chest yet again, "How can you not?"

He fought the urge to take hold of her. "If anything happened to you because of me…" He couldn't bring himself to finish that sentence.

"Grant," she said his name again, and it was as if his chest broke open at the sound. "Something's already happened. The fight's already here. If you're the one who can put a stop to whatever this is, you need to. You're on the right side of this—you know you are."

Of course he knew that. It's what made all the inaction, the looking the other way, the lame excuses so infuriating. But she was right—he'd felt unsettled ever since that day. If he was blisteringly honest with himself, he'd run. He'd told himself he was following the chief's orders, trusting Luke, protecting others because he knew something like this was bound to happen. Only he'd been lying to himself. He'd run. And he'd never been the type to run before.

Looking into her eyes, feeling the way she gazed at him, Grant found the conviction he needed. But it would cost him. Perhaps a whole lot.

"I have to go do whatever I can to stop this. Now, before they try something more than broken signs or windows to keep me quiet. They can be ruthless." They hadn't—yet—but Grant had little doubt they would if he didn't stand up to them. Right now, no matter what the sergeant's orders had been. No matter what the danger.

"God is more powerful. Right is more powerful."

He wanted to believe like that, but it felt beyond him at the moment. "I don't know how to protect you." It was more of a lament than a fact. It felt just as dangerous to leave her here and vulnerable as it was to go back to Billings. There were no safe options. "I've got to protect you."

"But you're the only one who can do this." She laid her hand softly atop his. "I'm not afraid. I thought I would be, and maybe some part of me ought to be, but I'm not." She managed a small smile. "That's new for me. And I think you're why."

Grant had been the kind of man to run straight toward the danger. To face down any enemy, to charge into battle no matter the opponent. He'd lost that for a moment, but he'd found it again today. Because today, he wasn't just choosing to fight, he was recognizing who he was fighting *for*.

There was probably some poetic thing he ought to say, some cleverly worded declaration that fit the moment. Instead, Grant just reached out to her and pulled her to him.

Meg offered no resistance, none of the hesitation they'd each been fighting for so long. She laid her hands against his chest, and Grant wondered if she could feel the thundering of his heart under her palms. He looked down at her, wanting to be absolutely sure this was what she wanted. He tipped her chin up toward him, searching her eyes. It had to be her choice, not just his yearning.

She stood on her tiptoes, bringing her face closer to his. Even then, she didn't come to his chin, petite as she was. But it told Grant all he needed to know, and when he tipped his head down to meet her lips, it was like tumbling off the face of the earth. A heady, spinning descent that felt like soaring as much as falling. At that moment, he'd slay dragons, move mountains, do just about anything because of Meg. She was his courage. And maybe, just maybe, with the help of the faith she'd restored for him, that was all he needed.

The embrace was everything Meg had imagined and more. She knew, just by how he held

her, that she was as much a gift to him as he was
a gift to her. And the kiss? Well, every inch of
her felt the kiss. Meg couldn't say if her feet had
left the ground—it certainly felt as if she were
floating.

Grant had, in fact, lifted her to him with seem-
ingly no effort. For as big as he was, he could
be exquisitely tender. She'd always known this
Grant was inside the grumpy giant who'd stalked
into her diner a month ago, but he was so much
more. She'd sent Andy into battle, or into danger, many times. Still, this moment had deep
power. As if God had slowly, carefully led each
of them to this moment and to each other. She
knew, deeply, that the way toward the life she
wanted so badly to reclaim came through him.

The way Grant deepened the kiss told Meg
that the only way he could do what he needed to
do was if her heart went with him. She felt the
same. The only way she could send him to do it
was to know part of his heart stayed with her. It
might look like a risk on the outside, but on the
inside it felt like the most certain thing on earth.

When he finally pulled back to gaze at her
with wonder in his eyes, she felt dizzy and giddy.
"I thought we needed to call the police right
away."

Grant smirked—a completely new expression
that somehow made him even more handsome

than before—and said, "In another minute," then kissed her again. "And as you said before, I *am* the police."

Laughing, Meg let her head fall against his chest. What a wonder it was to stand near a battered door and broken glass and feel safe and loved. It was as if some enormous weight fell from her shoulders—one she hadn't understood she'd been carrying. She'd read countless Bible verses about how joy and peace could live in the face of strife and threat, but it was another thing altogether to *feel* it. To accept the help he gave, and to gladly give him the help he needed.

"Thank you," he said as he planted the gentlest of kisses to the top of her head.

"For what?" she said as she returned the soft kiss to the spot where she could feel his heart beating.

"For bringing me back to me. For bringing back what they tried to take from me. I didn't even realize it was gone. Just that I was…" He tightened his grip around her and Meg marveled in the sensation of his strength. "I don't know, lost?"

"Welcome home, Grant." It was true, in more ways than one. Still, it didn't address the deepest question. The one she feared asking. "*Are* you home?" She wanted him to be. So much. She wanted to have a future in High Mountain with this man.

He paused, letting Meg know he understood the weight and the true meaning of the question. "I know what my heart wants." He flushed, as if he found the words sentimental. "But there's so much we don't know. I don't want to put you through more uncertainty. The girls, too."

His care for the girls was so precious to her. It had been reluctant at first, but they'd won him over even before he realized it. "Some things are more certain than others."

Grant cocked his head quizzically. "Want to explain that?"

"There's all the other stuff—the details, the how's and where's and when's. Then there's the *true* stuff." She returned her hand to his chest and tapped his heart. "The certain-no-matter-what stuff. I have faith in our hearts. I have faith in God's faith in us. Too many things could have gone a million other ways, but they lined up to bring us together. That's not coincidence. That's God's hand." She needed to know. Before any of this went any further, she needed to know if Grant saw God in his life. She'd seen it clearly, but none of that mattered if he didn't. "Can you see that?"

His response was to feather a hand against her cheek. It was such a romantic thing, so out of character for him. "I can. You showed me." He laughed. "Well, Mom might argue she had a hand in it too. After all, she dragged me to church all those Sundays and swears there are elbow dents in my old bed from the nights she spent there praying for me."

Meg tucked herself against him more tightly. The air in the diner had been harsh and frightening when she'd come in this morning, but now it had the warm glow of sunrise filling the place. "A mother's prayers are a powerful thing."

She felt Grant's chest expand with a sigh. "I don't know what's ahead," he said. "I'm returning in direct violation of an order. I'm going to have to testify. I don't know how they know what I know, but it tells me that my sergeant has most likely tipped off whoever is at the top behind this." He paused before adding, "I can't trust him. I don't think I can trust anyone. I feel like I'll be heading back into a pit of snakes."

It was going to cost him a lot to go back and expose the corruption. Meg wondered what it was going to cost her as well. Time with Grant, obviously, because he needed to go back to Billings. But it was going to cost her a sense of security—things for Grant could go any number of ways, good or bad. God was going to have to go before him through this in big ways. *Protect him, Lord*, Meg prayed as she tightened her arms around him.

"When will you go?" she asked.

He pulled away to look into her eyes, lifting a lock of hair that had fallen onto her cheek. "As soon as possible. Today, if I can manage it." He cast his gaze beyond her to the damage. "I want to make sure this is all taken care of. And the farm. And I want to say goodbye to the girls."

His goodbye had too much weight to it. It told her how much Tabitha and Sadie meant to him, and the pain of it pierced her heart. Could it really be a permanent goodbye? She made herself ask, "Tell me the truth—how much danger are you in?" Part of her didn't want to know. Another part of her knew it was time to face this head on.

"Hard to tell. They could finish off my career if they wanted to. Push me out of the force in some kind of trumped-up disgrace. Make it too nasty to stay. I'll be careful, but I don't think we can rule out something more…physical. These types don't have any kind of code. If harming me—or worse—protects them, they may not think twice." He held her gaze, regret in his eyes. "How can I ask you to go through this? After all you've been through?"

Meg tried to return his gaze with all the courage she had. "I probably wouldn't have chosen it. I tried not to, actually. But my heart had other ideas. If you haven't noticed, I have a very strong and stubborn heart. And a big piece of it is going to Billings with you."

Grant cupped her chin. "That will make all the difference."

"What do we do now?"

"We call the police. We get this place and Mom's gate fixed up. We figure out what to tell the girls about why I'm going to be gone for a while. And I go try to take down a bunch of dirty cops and live to tell you all about it."

The last line was supposed to be a joke, but neither of them considered it so.

Chapter Twenty

A week later, Grant touched his finger to the picture of what he'd come to think of as his family—a cheery shot of Mom, Meg and the girls surrounded by puppies. *Let me come back to them, Lord.*

The prayers had come easier in the past week—either out of desperation or the rekindling of faith. Either reason worked. The prayers worked, too. They gave him peace and courage as he navigated his careful way here in Billings through dozens of closed-door meetings, inquiries, dark looks, and phone calls. His sergeant was angry, but Grant was okay with that. He held steadfast in the knowledge that he was where he needed to be, doing what he needed to be doing.

The outcome of all this? Well, that one was going to have to be God's territory. There were too many pieces of this puzzle that he couldn't see and wouldn't know. His part was to reveal what he knew, offer the evidence he had, and try not to think about who was plotting any payback for what he'd done.

Maybe it wasn't so much his prayers as the ones he knew Meg was sending up daily back in High Mountain. He hoped God took both in equal measure. *I already miss them so much.*

The past days had given him the answer to Meg's question—the one that morning in the diner amid the broken glass. Billings was no longer home. High Mountain had become—or maybe once again become—his home. What he fought for now, in addition to the justice he hoped would prevail, was the chance to go back there in peace. To hold his head high in the knowledge that he'd done what had to be done. The consequences— well, he wouldn't get to know those just yet.

What Grant did know was that he loved Meg. He knew that as certain as he knew all the facts and details he had submitted to Internal Affairs in advance of today's hearing. The trick now was to get the chance to tell her.

A knock came on the conference room door. "They're ready for you, Officer Emerson."

Grant pulled himself up to his full height, grabbed his thick notebook and nodded. "Let's go."

The following Friday, Cay pushed through the diner doors with a wide smile on her face. "Did you get it? Did you get Grant's text?"

Meg smiled. "I did." But given the wording of Grant's text, Meg could be certain he didn't send the same text to both of them. Grant's text had words just for her. Words that kept her heart beating faster all morning in anticipation of his truck pulling up in front of the diner.

Cay sat down on the counter stool Meg now thought of as "Grant's stool."

"I'm so glad all of this is over. I'm almost glad he didn't tell me what was going on. I'd have been so scared for him. I'm still worried about him, but I'm so proud, too."

Grant had told Meg he would inform his mother of some of the details of the corruption case, but not all of them. He said he had confided more to her, but Meg suspected that he hadn't shared the full extent of the case with her, either. What she did know frightened her. Still, she found solace in how Grant told her over and over that he was doing all he could to protect the people he cared about up here in High Mountain. "The people I care about"—he'd used those words, and they'd lodged themselves warm and comforting in Meg's heart. Even in the midst of his risks, he made her feel safe and loved.

"Have you told the girls?" Cay asked. "I imagine they'll be eager to see him. We're *all* eager to see him." She gave that last statement a conspiratorial look. In the time that Grant had been back down in Billings, Cay—and both her sisters, to be honest—had tried mightily to get Meg to admit to a romance with Grant.

Meg thought about admitting it to Cay. Grant was due to walk through the door any moment now, and she was sure she wouldn't be able to hide her feelings when he did. Still, she ought to at least try and let things unfold with his mother on Grant's terms, even if she was unlikely to succeed at doing anything but throwing her arms around the man within seconds of his arrival.

"They're in school. I'll let them know later." Meg stacked menus with what she hoped was an ordinary air.

"Oh, yes, later. After you've had a chance to say a *proper hello*."

Maybe there was no point in keeping anything from Cay. She clearly already knew. "Coffee and pie while you wait?" she suggested, reaching for the pot. Her eye caught the extra-large mug reserved for Grant under the counter as she reached for one to place in front of Cay. How good it would feel to fill that big mug up again and watch the appreciation warm Grant's eyes.

"Don't you know it," Cay replied, nodding toward the peach pie under the dome on the counter.

Just after Meg finished serving Cay, the diner phone rang. "Good morning, Sundial Diner."

"I'm out back in the alley." Grant's voice sent sparks down her spine. Meg started to reply, but he went on, "Don't say anything. I saw Mom's car and, well, let's just say I'd prefer a more private welcome. Can you make an excuse to come out back?"

Flustered, amused and downright intrigued, Meg somehow found a casual voice to sputter, "Of course, sir. Just give me a moment." She hung up the phone and said, "Delivery out back," to Mike and Cay.

"I can get it," Mike offered.

"Oh, no, I'm fine," Meg replied quickly. She fought the urge to check her hair and makeup in the reflection of the glass cabinets, willing her feet to take unhurried steps out the now-repaired back door.

A strong set of arms grabbed her instantly, pulling her to one side out of view as the door closed behind her. And then she was in Grant's arms, lost in a kiss that was both tender and fierce at the same time. A kiss that spoke of how desperately long the days apart had been. How important they'd become to each other. It was just an average, slightly grimy back alley, but it felt like paradise to be there with him.

"I've missed you," he breathed into her hair when they finally managed to speak.

"We've all missed you," she replied, the coil of

worry and tension over his absence—and what he was doing while absent from High Mountain—finally beginning to unwind.

One dark eyebrow raised. "All of you?" There was a warm laughter in his words.

She smiled up at him. "Well, some of us more than others. Some of us have missed you a whole lot."

"Am I allowed to be glad to hear that?" He seemed less tense, less burdened than he had been when he left. How could he not? He'd gone up against the injustice like David against Goliath, and come away with what seemed like a victory. Who knew how complete, or for how long, but he had returned as the man who didn't back down from a fight. Meg didn't think it was overdramatic to say that it had restored his soul.

"I give you permission to be delighted." She loved him. She'd known that almost since the night he decided to return to Billings, but somehow this didn't seem like the right time to say something that important. A declaration of love shouldn't be stolen in some back alley like a kiss under the high school bleachers.

"I have two really important things to say." Grant looked around. "Lousy setting, I know, but I had to improvise, and I wasn't willing to wait."

"It's not *so* lousy," she offered, trying to ignore the dumpster beside them and the dust piled up in one corner. "We found the puppies here, didn't we?"

"There's my optimist."

It was delectable to hear him say "my." They *did* belong to each other. Why had they wasted so much time trying to ignore that? Meg wrapped her arms around his neck, marveling in how his eyes shone all the more when she did. Those eyes were still a deep steel gray, but they had so much light behind them now. "So…" she cued, sure she was grinning wildly. "Just two things, huh?"

"Two really important things." He pulled away to look at her but didn't release his hold on her one bit. "One is that I'm coming home. For good. I turned in my resignation from the Billings force this morning."

She knew what that had cost him. "Grant…"

"It was an easy decision. After everything that happened, my loyalty was gone. They wanted me out of there. And I couldn't stand the thought of staying, wishing I was here."

"What will you do?"

Grant looked up at the sky for a moment. "I don't know. I don't know what I'm going to do or how or…for crying out loud, I don't even know where I'm going to live up here."

"Oh, I have a feeling your Mom will take you in."

He grimaced. "Not a long-term solution. For

one thing, I'm thirty-two and my feet hang over the edge of the bed."

She tightened her arms around him, wallowing in his long-term thinking. "All solvable." Still, it would be so lovely to have him right next door, to see him walking across the fields toward her and the girls. To know he was so close nearby.

"I know," he agreed. "After all, someone once told me there's all the other stuff—the how's and where's and when's. Then there's the *true* stuff. And that's the second thing."

Meg didn't respond. She couldn't.

"The other thing, the true stuff, is that I need you in my life. I need the girls. I need my family and even the confounded dogs. I need all of this way more than anything I thought I needed back in Billings." He dipped his forehead to touch hers, something so intimate and tender it took her breath away. "Because I love you. I've got a whole bunch of words like impossible and implausible and irrational and unlikely, but not one of them changes the fact that I love you. And I want to be here, figuring it all out with you. For you. For us."

"Well, what do you know?" she whispered.

"What?" he asked, puzzled.

"Just a minute ago I was thinking you can't

profess love in a stolen moment in a back alley. Turns out I was wrong."

He laughed. Easily. Heartily. "So it's mutual?"

"Like you wouldn't believe." And she kissed him, just to make sure he knew how wonderfully, blessedly mutual it was.

Epilogue

Meg smiled at Grant and Cay as she scooped out another generous helping of ice cream. "I can't think of a better way to spend the Fourth of July."

Grant continued to stack paper bowls next to her. "I wouldn't be surprised if Pastor Jim asks the farm to host this every year."

"There might come a time when there are too many animals on the farm to pull this off," Cay replied, "But it sure feels good now." In fact, the farm field was filled with children running, dogs barking, and a generally joyful picnic dinner to celebrate the holiday.

Dr. Vicky walked up with Taylor on one hip. "The dogs look great," she remarked. "Daisy's going to need a bigger set of wheels soon. Chocolate, please."

Cay laughed as she handed Vicky a bowl of chocolate ice cream, winking as she doused it with a heap of sprinkles. "That's just what I need—a faster Daisy. She's too fast for me as it is." As if to prove her point, Daisy sped by chased by Tabitha and Sadie and a pack of other children. "I'd be lying if I didn't say how much I enjoy all the commotion." She pinched the child's cheek. "Are you going to share your mama's ice cream or do you get your own?"

Vicky chuckled. "I've only got so many hands. We'll share." She gave a wave as she walked off to where a group of picnic tables had been set up for the big barbecue dinner that had just concluded.

Peggy walked up, a wide smile on her face. "Cay," she said as she pointed to the container of strawberry, "I've got some great news, I think."

Meg scooped out a helping of strawberry for the woman while Cay asked, "What? Tell me."

Peggy leaned in. "Well, I can't say for certain yet, but I think maybe Carly is coming home."

Cay grabbed Peggy's hand. "Really? Peggy, that's wonderful."

Peggy shook her head. "I was so sad to see her go. Running away from your problems never does seem to work, does it?"

"I hope she comes home to you, Aunt Peggy," said Grant. "You tell her I said High Mountain is a good place to come home to."

Meg stole a glance at Grant. The position he'd taken as one of High Mountain's four police officers didn't pay as much as his post in Billings, but some things were worth far more than money. He'd transformed right in front of her eyes from the gruff man who darkened her diner door four months ago. And his steadfast devotion to her had transformed her as well. If there had ever been a doubt High Mountain was Grant's true home, it was long gone.

Such a great big happy day, Meg thought to herself. *I'm so grateful.*

When almost all the ice cream had been dished out, Grant grabbed Meg's hand. "Mom, mind if I borrow Meg for a moment?"

Cay grinned. "Not a bit. I think I've got the sugar rush under control here."

Grant pulled on Meg's hand. "Let's take a walk."

He led her to the shade of one of the farm's largest trees, an ancient-feeling thing boasting long branches spread wide with lush leaves. The dappled sunlight streaming down through the foliage played across his face as Grant took her in his arms. "Happy Fourth," he said as he hoisted her up to sit on one of the lower branches.

"Same to you." It was amusing to look down on him when he spent so much time towering over her.

"A little bird told me tomorrow is your birthday."

That had to be Tabitha and Sadie's doing. "It is."

"I'd make you a cake, but that's pretty much out of my skill set."

She ran a hand through his hair. "You have other gifts." He'd become such a marvelous part of her and the girls' lives she couldn't imagine how they'd ever been happy without him. Safe and loved indeed.

His eyes warmed even further at her touch. "Funny you should say that. I have a birthday gift for you."

"Early?"

He shrugged. "Today seemed like a good day to give this particular gift to you."

"You won't hear me complain. I love birthday gifts."

"I hope you love this one." With that, Grant reached into his pocket and produced a small black box. "And I hope you'll say yes." He tilted the box open to reveal a delicate vintage diamond solitaire. Meg grabbed Grant's shoulder to keep from sliding off the branch. "This was my grandmother's. My grandfather asked her to marry him under this very tree. Figured it was a tradition worth keeping. Will you marry me, Meg?"

Meg nearly fell off the limb in the best of ways, sliding into his arms. "Yes!"

He set her on the ground and slipped the ring onto her finger. There was something wonderful in how it fit perfectly. How everything had fallen into place in ways she'd never hoped could happen. Grant kissed her as if they had all the time in the world together—and in a way, they did. A whole new life seemed to spread itself before her, before them.

Before all of them. "How should we tell the girls?"

Grant grinned. "I told Mom to send them over after ten minutes."

Meg turned to see Tabitha and Sadie—complete with Daisy and Sam in tow—dashing across the field toward them. "You were sure I'd say yes, were you?"

He smiled and took her hand. "Some risks aren't risks at all."

* * * * *

Dear Reader,

Welcome to High Mountain and Three Sisters Rescue Farm! From the moment Cay, Peggy and Barb announced themselves and their dream for the farm in my imagination, I knew we were in for a marvelous time. As each of these sisters watches (and meddles) as their children's lives are changed through the power of faith and love. It's more than just the animals who find rescue.

Meg and Grant are sure they don't need each other. Of course, the sisters—and Meg's adorable daughters—have other ideas. It's my prayer that their journey toward love offers you hope in whatever challenges you face.

Many thanks to Mike Rabinowitz for his help getting the law enforcement details right.

Come back to High Mountain in the next book, where Peggy's daughter, Carly, discovers the healing of a homecoming...and some sweet rabbits join the inhabitants of Three Sisters Rescue Farm.

Blessings,
Allie

   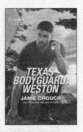